The
Fire-Raiser

The
Fire-Raiser

MAURICE GEE

HOUGHTON MIFFLIN COMPANY
Boston

Text copyright © 1986 by Maurice Gee
First American edition 1992
Originally published in New Zealand in 1986 by Penguin Books

www.houghtonmifflinbooks.com

The text of this book is Galliard.

Library of Congress Cataloging-in-Publication Data
Gee, Maurice.
The Fire-raiser / by Maurice Gee.
p.   cm.
Summary: In 1915 Kitty Wix and her friends try to stop the arsonist who is terrifying their small New Zealand town.
HC ISBN: 0-395-62428-2   PB ISBN: 0-618-75041-X
[1.Arson—Fiction. 2. New Zealand—Fiction. 3. Mystery and detective stories.]
I. Title.
PZ7.G2578Fi 1992   92-8017
[Fic]—dc20   CIP   AC

HC ISBN-13: 978-0-395-62428-9
PA ISBN-13: 978-0-618-75041-2

Printed in the United States of America
HAD 10 9 8 7 6 5 4 3 2 1

Contents

CHAPTER ONE

The Red Balaclava

THE JESSOP FIRE-RAISER had been quiet for almost three months. Some in the town believed nothing more would be heard of him. Others held the opinion that his last fire had so nearly got away and destroyed the row of houses behind the church that he had become frightened, perhaps that he felt remorse and would give himself up one day and ask forgiveness for his sins from God. The vicar of All Saints, the church burned to the ground on Christmas night, 1914, held that opinion. He was wrong. All of them were wrong. The man with the fire in his head — so Thomas Hedges, headmaster of Jessop Main School, described him — had drawn back to make a better jump. He had reached the point where he wanted to burn a building with some live thing inside.

On the night of 23 March 1915, he was out again. As usual, he had not waited until the town was asleep. He liked to see large crowds at his fires and taste their fear. He hugged himself at such times. He bit the insides of his cheeks to stop himself from shouting his delight. Light and flame, which he found glorious, bathed him like water and made him newborn. So he was out just after 10 o'clock on the twenty-third, creeping through the lanes and alleys of Jessop, by hedges and board fences, by park and riverbank, sack on his shoulder, black baggy coat lapping his ankles, and red balaclava tight on his head. No one saw him, no one had a glimpse. He threaded his way into the town as though on tracks only he knew. He was a big man, agile, strong. When he came to the fence at the back of Dargie's Livery Stables he hefted his sack over with one hand and set it down on the other side, then vaulted after it like a boy. For a moment he crouched in shadows, looking at the building, the roof tall as a church, the weatherboards warped by forty years of Jessop sun. He loved that old timber. It would burn like kindling wood. Then he ran to the door of the office where old Dargie sat all day, joking with his grooms, and broke it open with a pinchbar from his sack. He went through the room in three strides, but opened the door carefully on the other side. He did not want to alarm the horses.

The big shed at Dargie's was ninety feet long. The darkness in its ceiling was like a cloud and the fire-raiser gave it an anxious glance, as though it might open and pour down rain and douse his fire. The windows on the street side let in light from the gas lamp outside Wix's bakery. It made the grain sacks gleam like fat gold ingots and the straw on the floor like golden thread. It caught the name 'Dargie' on buggies and carts, and shone on chains and harness and the worn leather of horse collars and the iron rims of wheels. It lit the rungs of the ladder going up to the loft at the far end of the shed, where a fringe of hay hung down like a beard below a mouth. Along the left-hand wall were a dozen horse stalls, but the light was blocked by wooden doors and the fire-raiser could not see how many were occupied. He heard a snicker though, and the stamp of a hoof in straw, and it made him smile. Dargie's business was going downhill as motorcars and lorries took the place of horses, but the fire-raiser guessed that five or six animals were stabled tonight. He had nothing against horses. He liked horses, but a time had come when his fire must consume life. The horses were not important. Outrage, power, pleasure, were important.

He reached into the pockets of his coat and hauled out handfuls of cotton waste, and into his sack for rags, old shirts, old dresses. These he stuffed into cracks and crevices, into the buggies, the feed sacks, working fast, with an eye gleaming now and then at the office and the high double doors to the street. Once a cart rumbled by, hooves went clop on the road, and the carter whistled *Bonnie Jean*. The fire-raiser squatted in a hollow until the sounds were gone. He grinned with elation as he crept out, and licked his lips and cleared his throat and spat in the hay. He felt he had rubbed shoulders with the town and picked its pocket. From his sack he took a gallon can of benzine. He unscrewed the cap and tossed it away and poured the liquid on hay and rags and grain sacks. It gleamed like glass and gurgled like a tap. A horse in the nearest stall snorted and the white of its eye showed over the door. The fire-raiser snarled, 'You can squeal all you want in a minute.'

He saved a quarter gallon — sloshed it in the can to make sure — and climbed the ladder to the loft like a spider in a web. Hay lay thick up there, springy under his feet, and he fluffed it up before splashing it with benzine. He threw the can further back in the loft where it boomed softly and made the horse snicker again. 'Shuddup!' he said. He took a box of matches from his coat and rattled it — the sound of matches made him lick his lips — and chose one, felt its beautiful round head and dry wood stem. Matches were magical to him and full of secret whispers, promises. He scratched it on the box and flame sprang out. The red balaclava bloomed like a rose. He let the matchstick burn, knowing the power in his hand, and when the flame had nothing more to feed on, thrust it like a gift into the hay. Flame filled the inside of his head. It ran along his arteries. It licked around his bones. He gave a whinnying scream, like a horse, and capered in a dance, swimming in the red and yellow light. Then he seized a torch of hay and leaped with it flaming in his hand, with his black coat flapping, down to the hay pile in the shed, and rolled in it, setting it on fire, and ran along the wall, touching things as though with a wand, waking them up. Flames ran like snakes. He kept up with them, whooping. Horses reared and screamed in their stalls. He came to the double doors and burst them open and stood in the entrance, looking at the furnace he had made. Then he raised one arm, with fingers hooked, saluting, and gave a soundless yell, and vanished into the night. In Dargie's Livery Stable the fires leaped and the horses screamed.

◆

It was late for Irene Chalmers to be up, and late for Noel and Kitty Wix, but bedtime was not a fixed part of Phil Miller's day. He went when he felt like it and most nights was out in the streets of Jessop, round the pub doors, watching the night life. Phil was the son of Charlie Miller, tally clerk once, and then a drunkard, and over the hill now at White's Landing working in the sawmill and living in the camp. Phil lived alone. He scavenged and ran errands, delivered this and that, and picked up things he claimed were lying about. He wasn't a thief, though he got close, or a vagabond either. Nor was he a schoolboy, although he went to school, barefoot, three days out of five. If asked, he would have called himself a Port boy. At Jessop Main School his gang was Port Rats. They had a running war with the River Rats.

Phil heard the alarm for Dargie's fire and saw the glow in the sky and beat the brigade there. He was one of the first to arrive, coming into the street just as the mayor's car stopped. If he had looked he would have seen Irene Chalmers in the back, and that would have made him curl his lip. Maybe he would have shouted some insult, or spat on the car. He could spit twenty feet. But the fire was well alight, leaping in windows, and Wix the baker was rescuing horses and Phil ran to help. So Irene Chalmers, 'Charmy-Barmy', was spared his contempt.

Irene had been to the Princess to see *Bronco Billy's Wild Ride*. Mrs. Chalmers found the movies vulgar and was telling her husband so as they drove home. They were not going to that sort of thing again. Irene didn't listen. This went on all the time and she had learned to float away until her name came up. Then she got very sharp and clever, and stayed very quiet, just putting in coughs and sniffs when they were needed. If she did it right she could make her father stand up to her mother, make him tell her, 'Leave the child alone'. Tonight she let it go on like voices in a bedroom, and she replayed little pieces of Bronco Billy. She had been enthralled. Even bald old Trumbull thumping on the piano had caught her up, although she knew the easiness of what he was doing. Bronco Billy crouched on his horse's neck while arrows whistled by, and gallopy-gallopy-gallop went the piano. Then, somehow, she was at a fire, and real horses stood on their hind legs, and her father was running down the road. Phil Miller was there — 'Fleabites' he was called — and no doubt he was to blame. She wanted to see better and she got out of the car and ran after her father until she felt her face go hot with fire. Her mother caught her and tried to take her back, but too many people were in the way, and her mother got interested too. They stood in front of Wix's shop and watched. Irene was able to say next day she was one of the first to see the fire.

But Kitty Wix discovered it. Kitty Wix was first. Normally her father baked early in the morning, but now and then a special order came from White's Landing — loaves and pies for logging gangs on special contract — and he baked at night so the carrier could load up at daybreak. Kitty and her brother, Noel, sometimes came to help. They were there, in the bakehouse, on the night of the fire. George Wix opened the oven and looked at the loaves at the very moment the fire-raiser was climbing into the loft. The baker was wearing an apron and a white cap, a costume that made him play the clown for his children. He was a brisk, plump man, given to snorts and whistles and exclamations of mock woe. Quotations bubbled from him, apt, inapt, and comic verse, or tragic verse given a comic inflexion. His tongue could not be still and seemed to bounce along in time with his hands, always busy. He peered at the loaves and cried, 'Lordy, Lordy! A smell of burning fills the startled air. Hand me that paddle, Noel. And bring your basket. You too, Kit, or else the multitudes will not be fed.'

He spilled out the hot loaves and Noel humped his basket to the table and tipped them on a cooling tray and spread them out. Wix filled Kitty's basket. He tapped a loaf with his forefinger and listened like a doctor listening to a chest. 'You have baked me too brown, I must sugar my hair. Kitty love, leave those and run along home. And take a loaf for your Ma. Noel, stoke up. We can't leave White's Landing without 'umble pies.' He closed the oven door and hopped across to a bench, where he pummelled a great lump of dough with his fists. 'Off you go, Kit. Don't dawdle.'

Noel was feeding lengths of wood into the firebox. 'She's scared of the dark.'

'I am not,' Kitty said. 'I want the best loaf, that's all.'

'All Wix loaves are best loaves. Hurry, love. Your Ma'll be dropping her stitches.'

Kitty chose a loaf and wrapped it in her apron and held it to her stomach like a hot-water bottle.

'Tell her Noel won't be long. It's midnight for me. Who ne'er the mournful midnight hours — '

'Weeping on his bed has sate,' Kitty finished. 'You're silly, Dad.' She let herself out into the alley leading to Dargie Street. To tell the truth, she was scared of the dark, but the alley was lit by the gas lamp in front of the shop, so this part of the walk didn't worry her. She unwrapped a corner of the loaf and nibbled the crust, carefully, so her mother wouldn't notice. At the end of the alley she heard a strange noise. It seemed to be a sound of wind and a neighing of horses,

13

almost as if a gale was coming and horses were galloping ahead, escaping it. She stepped into Dargie Street and saw at once the windows of the stable all lit up. The double doors were wide, like oven doors, and from inside came a flickering like a magic-lantern show. She had no time to understand that the thing that flapped and loomed like a huge black bird was a man, running on the road, and his vulture skull a red balaclava, before he knocked her tumbling back into the alley mouth. Her loaf went flying and rolled in the gutter. She knelt on hands and knees, with her head poking into Dargie Street, and watched him run away out of the light with a long, wolfish, loping stride and one arm raised sideways, crooked, black, and the fist on it shining like an egg. His coat came to his ankles; it writhed and flapped. He seemed to her eight or nine feet tall. His balaclava gave him a round inhuman head. Then she heard the horses screaming, saw the flames, and scrambled to her feet and ran down the alley and burst in at the bakehouse door.

'Dargie's stables are on fire!' she screamed.

That was how Kitty Wix found the fire, and how George Wix was on the spot to save the horses. He sent Noel running to ring the firebell and sent Kitty knocking on doors for help. By the time she came back, all the horses were out. Phil Miller was holding one by the mane, even though it reared and lifted him off his feet. She ran to help. 'Easy, boy.'

'She's a mare,' Phil Miller said. He was so contemptuous, she came back at him, 'I saw the man who lit it.'

'Garn!'

'He knocked me over.'

'Knocked you silly.'

Thomas Hedges arrived, panting. 'I'll take her, Miller. Watch your feet, Kitty.' He had been in the observatory on Settlers Hill. It was his ambition to discover a comet and he spent long nights searching the sky. When the firebell rang, he used the small telescope to study the glow, and when he saw how big the fire was, he ran down to help. The mare reared as he took her and George Wix hurried up and tied a cloth round her eyes.

'A bad business, Mr. Hedges.'

'Are all the horses out?'

'She was the last. We'd better get them down to Fleming's yard.'

'Our friend again, I dare say.'

'I saw him,' Kitty said, but the men were leading the horses away, and the brigade was coming with a clangor, and no one heard. Mr. Chalmers, the mayor, was running about importantly, trying to make people move back. He flapped his hands up and down, he pushed as though pushing an invisible wall, but no one moved. Kitty felt sorry for Irene Chalmers, having such a feeble dad, but Irene, watching everything with her china-doll face, did not seem to care. She took no notice when her mother covered her ears so she would not hear a fireman swearing at his hose.

They coupled up, they ran the hoses as close to the building as they could come, and turned the water on and sent it hissing and crashing through windows and doors, but nothing was going to save Dargie's Livery Stables. The flames seemed wetter than the water and they poured everywhere, and were like a wind at the same time, slapping and thumping, puffing and beating. In the end they turned into a throat, gulping roof and walls. Great storm-clouds of smoke rolled up and vanished in the dark and sparks rode with them, swarms of busy flies. Noel, panting back through the streets after ringing the firebell, thought half the town was on fire and could not believe, when he turned into Dargie Street, that all that pulsing glow came from one fire. He was disappointed not be welcomed back as a hero. Nobody noticed him. He found Kitty and said, 'I got there. I rang the bell,' in a loud voice, but she said, 'Noel, I saw him! The man who lit it. He knocked me over,' and then, not pausing, 'Dad got the horses out. Me and Phil Miller helped.' He was bitter about being so far away, running alone through dark streets while that was going on. He watched a wall go crashing down and hoped nothing would be left of Dargie's.

The fire-raiser stood at the front of the crowd, further up the street. His mouth was open, tasting the fire. He had been one of the first to arrive, and though George Wix had saved the horses, he was not disappointed. This was his biggest fire yet. Bigger than the church, the barn, the shop, the derelict house. Almost as big as the fires he had dreamed of as a boy. He felt the fear around him, all of it a tribute. Horses in the flames would have been even better, but this was enough.

Chalmers came by and tried to move him back. He moved. Why not? He had to be part of everything. Another wall fell, with a whump and thump, and flames rolled like breakers and the sparks were like bees on fire. The fire-raiser laughed soundlessly. He gave mighty whoops in this skull. And stood in the crowd, a citizen of Jessop, watching the fire.

His balaclava was in his pocket, his pinchbar in his jacket, its curved handle snug in his armpit. His old coat was hidden under the bridge. He was a big man, middle aged, with green eyes and lumpy bones in his face. Some people thought he was good looking, others that he would be if he did not look sullen so much of the time. Kitty Wix, if she had seen him, would not have recognized him as the man who had bowled her over.

She and Noel went home, and George Wix lit his dead stove to bake the batch of pies for White's Landing — they would not be up to his usual standard. Chalmers, the mayor, drove his wife and daughter home and went back to Dargie's, but there was nothing he could do. Hedges went home, telling Phil Miller first that it was late for him to be wandering round and he'd better be off. He dreamed of comets that night. Phil Miller dreamed of rescuing horses and riding away on one, high into the mountains, into freezing snow and icy winds — but that was at four in the morning when the temperature always dropped and his thin blanket failed to keep him warm. The fire-raiser left soon after the mayor. That seemed the proper time. He was not interested in steam and ash and hosing down. He walked through the streets and over the bridge, where he forgot to collect his coat — his fire-coat, he thought of it, and the balaclava his fire-hat — and back to the sleeping farm in the bend of the river. He had a full, fat smile on his face. He would not need another fire for a while now. This one sat inside him like a meal. He would lie in his bed and digest it.

CHAPTER TWO

Miss Perez

PHIL MILLER, in holey pants and greasy shirt, was scavenging next morning in the ruins of the stables. He kept his bare feet clear of the hot ashes and kept a mound of rubble between him and the police sergeant, McCaa, and two of his constables, who were poking about where the loft had been. Phil was no favorite of theirs. He'd had more than one clip on the ear from McCaa.

Something black and round caught his eye. He pounced on it and rubbed it on the rolled-up black bundle under his arm, and saw it shine. A penny, still warm from the fire. He put it in his pocket and sent a look in McCaa's direction. They were excited along there and one of the constables was heaving at a beam. Phil took his chance to dig in a pile of ashes with a stick. Nothing there, but a shine of brass caught his eye across by a half-fallen wall and he worried out a carriage lamp from a tangle of scorched boards. It was as hot as a kettle and he was squatting by it, wondering if he could hide it and pick it up later, when the sergeant's shout bounced like a fist on his skull and the man was standing over him. He put up his arm to shield himself. 'Not doing anything, Sir. Just having a look.'

The sergeant hauled him to his feet by the back of his shirt. 'Pinching eh, young Miller? Got you this time.'

'No, Sir. Just looking.'

'What's this then?' He pulled the bundle from under Phil's arm and let it fall out to its full length. It was a coat, long enough, the sergeant thought, for a man on stilts. The buttons were gone and the collar was green with age, but once it had been a very good garment. 'Where'd you get it?' He sniffed the cloth. 'Not burnt, eh?'

'I found it,' Phil said. He did not expect to be believed.

'Pinched it, more like.'

'No, Sir. Found it just now. Under the footbridge.'

'What were you doing there?'

Phil told the truth. 'I went for a pee, Sir.'

'I catch you peeing boy, I'll skin you alive. Pee on your own place.'

'Yes, Sir.'

The sergeant grunted. He let Phil's shirt go and felt in the pockets of the coat and pulled out some threads of cotton waste.

'There was a bit more of that. I chucked it away,' Phil said.

'What else was there? What did you pinch?'

'Nothing.'

McCaa watched him suspiciously. As crooked as a creek, this boy, a real little jailbird in the making. He felt in the pockets again. 'Just lying on the ground there, eh?'

'No, Sir. It was rolled up. Sort of hidden.'

'How's that?'

'Up the top of the bank, under the boards. In some black-berries.'

The sergeant saw a blackberry leaf stuck to the cloth. He nodded. 'Did you see anyone hanging round down there?'

'No, Sir.' He wasn't going to say that two men, railway clerks, had seen him peeing and shouted at him.

'All right, I'll keep it,' McCaa said. 'Now you clear out, young Miller. Get to school. I see you here again you'll get a thick ear.'

He watched the boy hurry away, and thought sourly that in a year or two he'd be burgling houses. A pity he couldn't lock him up now and save himself trouble later.

He rolled up the coat and told his constables to keep busy and went down the road to George Wix's house. He'd spoken to the girl already and got nothing useful. He had learned not to trust stories from children, but she was very sure of herself, that miss. Perhaps she would recognize the garment. He spoke to her in the living room, with her mother and brother listening. The size of the coat, when he held it up, supported Kitty's story that the man had been big.

'It was all flapping round him, like wings.'

'And long like this?'

'Yes. Round his ankles. And he had the red thing on his head.'

'Balaclava,' Mrs. Wix said, knitting in her chair.

'His head was like a ball — you know, all round. And he ran funny.'

'How?'

'Like a horse. Kind of galloping.'

Noel made a sound of neighing and his mother leaned at

him and poked his rump with a knitting needle. 'That's enough from you. You're sure someone lit it, Sergeant?'

'We found a can, Mrs. Wix. Motor spirit. Dargie didn't keep any of that.'

'He had his arm up,' Kitty said. 'Like a club.'

'And he didn't look round? You didn't see his face?' McCaa said.

'No.'

'You're lucky,' Noel said. They all looked at him. He grinned and cut his throat with his finger.

'That's enough, Noel. You get off to school. Leave Kitty alone.'

'I think they can both go, Mrs. Wix. They did very well last night. I wish we had more like them.'

So the Wix children went to school, feeling pleased with themselves. They hoped Mr. Hedges would mention them in class. But Hedges, 'Clippy' Hedges, was in no mood to praise. He was mad as a bottle of ants, to use his own phrase. On his way to school he had dropped in for a word with Frau Stauffel, the piano teacher, and found her red-eyed from a night of weeping. She gave him a letter to read, and from the first sentence he had popped and fizzed.

Dear Madam,

I am writing to terminate Irene's piano lessons. Payment has been made to the end of the term and as we have no contract, I must ask you to refund the money at your earliest convenience. Irene will shortly be going away to a private school and will continue with her music there.

Yours faithfully,
Ann Chalmers

'You will not make repayment. You will not do it,' Hedges said.

'That is not important,' Frau Stauffel said.

'Payment is a contract. We'll take her to court.'

'But Thomas, it is not money I care for. It is Irenee. This woman, Ann Chalmers, she thinks music is for frilly girls to catch a husband. But this is not a girl, this is Irenee. She is *wunderkind* — '

'Now, my dear. You must not use that language.'

'It is my language. And his. And his.' She pointed to busts of Beethoven and Brahms on the mantelpiece. 'And Irenee is not some tickler of ivories. She is musician.'

'Yes, Lotte, yes. I'll see Mrs. Chalmers. I'll tell her Irene must have her chance.'

'To this woman I am Hun. I shall stomp on her with my piano.'

He left her thundering out a stomping tune, and was pleased that she had turned from tears to anger, but anger still fizzed in him as he faced his class and he shook his head at Irene as she came to the piano. He took out his tuning fork instead, and banged it on his desk and only began to simmer down when he heard its note. Hedges was a man who liked children, unlike many teachers he had known. He wasn't with his pupils long before a sense of expectation filled him, a sense of happy futures. He was oppressed as well by a knowledge of meanness, cruelty and pain, all waiting round corners, but he never let that bother him more than a mild headache or a bit of heartburn would have. He believed one must carry on as though life were the happy thing it could be. Children deserved no less.

He was a square-built man with an ugly face: nose like

plasticine dented by a thumb, eyes that went one this way, one that, but saw well enough, and mouth like a leather purse, full of crooked teeth. His skin was pitted from some childhood illness and one of his ears mauled as though by a cat. Children had been known to cry at the sight of him, but those in standard six, his class, were proud of his ugliness. He had been at Jessop Main School twenty years, five as headmaster.

The class sang *Men of Harlech,* then Hedges wagged his thumb at Irene and she trotted to the piano, bright and eager, and gave the keys her beautiful sure touch. She did not know, Hedges guessed, what her mother had done.

> *Hark hark the lark at Heaven's gate sings*
> *While Phoebus 'gins to rise . . .*

The playing was much better than the singing.

'There,' Hedges said, 'that's opened our lungs. Now we'll stretch our minds. Arithmetic.'

'Sir, Sir?' cried a boy called Bob Taylor.

'Yes, what is it?'

'Some British ships got sunk in the Dardanelles.'

'And some French,' Kitty Wix said.

'The Turks are floating mines down with the current,' Noel Wix said.

'I know, Wix. I'm glad to see you're reading the newspaper. Arithmetic.'

'Sir,' Phil Miller said, 'the British captured Neuve Chapelle.' He pronounced it 'Newve Chapple'.

'Neuve. Neuve. Watch my lips. Neuve Chapelle. That's here.' Hedges strode to the wall-map, which was pinned with flags in a crooked line. He shifted one a quarter inch. 'But you see, it's no real advance . . .' He stopped and faced the class, and grinned. 'Nearly, but not quite. Get your books out.'

'Did you see the fire, Sir?' Taylor said.

'Why did Mr. Wix cover up the horses' eyes?' Irene asked.

'So they couldn't see the flames.'

'They could hear them, Sir.'

'A horse's brain works differently. It's smaller than the human brain, compared with its body size.'

'Their heads are bigger, Sir,' Phil Miller said.

'But the cranial cavity. . .' Hedges tapped his head. Then he sighed. He knew very well what was happening, and liked it more than arithmetic. A principle of his teaching was to grasp children at the moment of their interest, and he saw interest in his class right now as well as cunning. 'All right. Arithmetic later. Miller. Wix. Ask Miss Perez if she'll step down.'

'Yes, Sir.'

'Yes, Sir.'

'Walk, if you don't mind. And ask politely. She's a lady who's used to ceremony.'

Phil and Noel ran in the corridor. Phil, barefooted, reached the steps to the belfry first. They were not friends. Phil was a Port Rat and Noel a River Rat.

'Quit shoving.'

'You shouldn't wear shoes, Wix. They slow you down.'

They scrambled up the narrow stairs and Phil opened the green-painted door at the top. The belfry was a little room, ten feet square, with a bell-tower like a chimney on top. The rope hung down, greasy with years of handling, and was looped over a nail in the wall. A clutter of junk filled the room: old desks, old slates, Indian clubs, hoops, broken bats, deflated footballs, mops and buckets, maps and charts, a dented trumpet, a kettle drum. Phil threaded through and came to a tall cupboard in a corner. Like the door, it was tongue-and-groove and painted green. It looked like a coffin standing on end. Phil took a key from a nail. He swallowed and waited till Noel was at his side.

'You open, eh?'

'Sure,' Noel said, and took the key. He was nervous too, but was not going to show it. He opened the cupboard and they looked at Miss Perez. She glimmered at them, smiling, with her head bent in a regal way. Her slender feet were in line with their knees, her hands, palm up, at her waist, seemed to offer, but the rest of her, so empty, seemed to want.

'I wonder if she was pretty?' Noel whispered.

'She was probably fat. With a face like Hedges.' Phil felt better, saying that. He reached in and took the frame that held the skeleton upright. 'Grab it lower down. Come on, don't stand there!'

They lifted out Miss Perez and side-stepped with her through the desks and hoops. Going down the stairs, they carried her like a bed, Phil at the head, Noel at the feet, but stood her up, remembering ceremony, for her entry into Hedges' room. The class sighed, and groaned, and gave a hiss of fear. Hedges, though, wouldn't have any nonsense. If Miss Perez was going to cause awe, he meant it to be as a fine piece of engineering. His first job was to demystify her.

'This is my good friend, Miss Perez. She apologizes for her state of undress.'

'Is that really her name, Sir?' Kitty Wix asked.

'Certainly, Kitty. I met her on an Amazon River steamer in '98. She was a Spanish lady, a singer at the Manaos Opera. She threw herself into the river for hopeless love of an Italian tenor.'

'Did she drown, Sir?' Irene asked.

'The piranhas ate her. Savage little fish. When we got her out, this is the way she was. Picked clean. If you look closely you can see teeth marks on her bones. The Italian tenor was so upset he sang an aria. It made us all cry. Then I bought her from the captain for seven shillings.'

Kitty grinned. 'That's all lies, Sir.'

'It's a kind of truth, Kitty. When we know nothing we're entitled to invent. But now — look at this, see the lovely way she's put together. The variety of movements she makes is matched by the variety of her joints. This one here — ' he touched her elbow — 'is a hinge joint. See how it rolls.'

He pulled a lever on the frame supporting Miss Perez and her forearm came up. The class gave a cry, half shock, half excitement. Hedges ignored it. He demonstrated the movement again. 'And there's a pivot joint that goes with it, so we can get another movement. See. Like that. Up and down we go, and then we twist. Marvelous, eh?'

'You were going to tell us about brains,' Irene said.

'So I was. Miss Perez could keep us busy for days. For a lifetime. Her loveliness increases — '

'Sir,' Irene complained.

'I'm sorry. The brain. You see how big this space is? I could get both my fists in if I tried. But a horse's brain wouldn't be much bigger than one fist. The human brain weighs three pounds. Think of three pounds of butter — '

'It would melt, Sir,' Noel said.

'Three pounds of mince. That would be better. And every little particle crammed with cells, taking information in, sending instructions out, making all your senses work, and muscles. Making you laugh and cry and think. Let me see. The brain is a hive with millions of bees, and your body is a garden full of flowers, a farm with clover and butter-cups . . . No, no, mustn't get poetic.' He scratched his head.

'Why not, Sir?' Kitty said. She'd been enjoying it.

'Sir,' Irene said, 'Miss Perez has got a very round head.'

'Yes, she has.' Hedges felt the shape with both hands. 'Some people would say that shows she's musical. This little bump here — ' he put his finger on a bulge above the skull's ear hole — 'represents harmony. But of course, phrenology isn't a science any more than astrology is.'

'Would the fire-raiser have a bump?' Noel asked.

'If we believed in it, Wix, he certainly would. Destruc-tiveness is here — ' he touched the place — 'very close to music, strangely enough. But it's nonsense. All we can say is, whoever lights those fires has got dark things in his mind. Or perhaps his mind is full of flames. Now that's a science, a brand new science called psychology.'

'Would Germans have a special-shaped head?' Phil asked.

'They've got square heads,' Bob Taylor said.

'Rubbish, Taylor,' Hedges said.

'That's what my dad says.'

'Your dad is wrong.'

'If that's a lady, Sir,' Kitty said, 'she should have one more rib than you.'

'Who told you that, Kitty?'

'God made Eve out of Adam's rib.'

27

'It's in the Bible,' Irene said.

'You mustn't believe everything you read in the Bible, Irene.'

'Mr. Hedges!' cried a voice from the door. Noel and Phil had left it open and Mrs. Bolton stood there, framed like a photograph. She was the senior woman teacher on the staff, and Hedges stalked in her life with cloven hoof. She saw herself as locked in battle with him, fighting for Christian behavior, right belief of every kind. She was appointed saviour, she believed, of Jessop's children. It was the main cause in her life, and she would not have had Hedges out of the school for anything.

'Mr. Hedges!'

'Ah, Mrs. Bolton. Captain Nemo welcomes you aboard.' He pulled a lever and the skeleton's hand came up in a wide-fingered salute.

Mrs. Bolton was not affronted, not afraid. She looked through Captain Nemo/Miss Perez. 'I heard you, Mr. Hedges. I'm not going to take it any further in front of the children, but I shall have a word with Reverend Wilmott.'

'Perhaps you and he would like to count the Captain's ribs?'

'You told us she was Miss Perez, Sir,' Kitty cried.

'Ah, Kitty, she can be whoever we want. Remember what I told you, we're entitled to invent. Now I think I'd better take the lady for some tea. Mrs. Bolton has some things she'd like to say.'

He picked up the skeleton and left the room. The class gave a sigh and made a desk-rattle of satisfaction.

'Quiet, children!' Mrs. Bolton cried. 'Settle down.' She drew in her breath, settled on them damply, weightily.

'Arms folded. Shoulders back. I want to talk about our patriotic pageant. Mr. Wilmott and I have finished the words.
We have a title now: Britannia Awakes! That is not to say
she ever slept. Yesterday I had some gratifying news. Mr.
Jobling, our Member of Parliament, will attend. And the
proceeds will go to the Belgian Relief Fund.'

'Where will we do it?' someone asked.

'In St. Andrews hall. In three weeks' time, which is not
enough. Not nearly enough, but that's when Mr. Jobling
can get here. So, we must throw ourselves into it. There are
songs to learn and costumes to make. And today I want to
choose the speaking parts. Sit up straight.'

The class obeyed. Most of them were eager to be in the
pageant. But they already knew who would get the best
parts.

'Britannia. We must have someone who stands up like a
soldier, who can use her voice. So — Kitty Wix.'

'Thank you, Mrs. Bolton,' Kitty squeaked. Her voice had
never seemed very big to her.

'Only because you are taller than Irene Chalmers. Britannia is tallest. You must keep your head up and your neck
straight. And never smile. I don't like the way you show
your teeth all the time, Kitty.'

'I'm sorry, Mrs. Bolton.'

'Now, Irene.' She gave her favorite a touch on the head.
'Gallant Little Belgium, brave and beautiful.'

Irene went pink and then went white. She loathed Mrs.
Bolton, who was always patting her and telling her how
nicely she spoke, and stood, and chewed, and kept her fin-
gernails and played the piano. The last was what angered
her most — to have Mrs. Bolton talking about music as

though it were no more important than good manners and dressing properly. Irene stared at her fingers and didn't say thank you. She heard Melva Dyer in the next desk whispering that Charmy-Barmy was going to cry, she thought she was getting Britannia. It wasn't true! She wanted to be nothing in Bolter's pageant. She didn't even want to sing in the chorus.

'Next,' Mrs. Bolton said, 'New Zealand. We need a big strong boy with shoulders back and nice clean teeth. Not you Wipaki, someone white. Wix! New Zealand! Heart of Oak!' Her face swelled with emotion. She put her hand on the table to steady herself.

'Who's going to be the Kaiser, Mrs. Bolton?'

'Not me.'

'Not me.'

'The Kaiser is a most important role,' Mrs. Bolton said. 'He doesn't have to act much, just pull faces. Miller, stand up.'

'I don't want to be the Kaiser, Mrs. Bolton.'

'Don't argue with me, Miller. Pull a face. Make some sort of nasty noise, boy.'

'I can't, Mrs. Bolton.'

To Noel, sitting a couple of desks away, it seemed that Phil was going to cry. He saw the greedy look on Bob Taylor's face and knew what Phil would lose by being Kaiser or breaking down. It puzzled him that he should feel as if it were happening to himself. He didn't like Phil Miller. His clothes stank for one thing, and he was always skiting and belching and twisting the arms of kids smaller than himself. But he felt if Bolters made him Kaiser it would be some bit of torture, done on purpose. He stuck his arm in the air and climbed to his feet. 'Mrs. Bolton, I'll be Kaiser. I can do faces.'

'I've already chosen you for New Zealand.'

'You watch, Mrs. Bolton.' He went cross-eyed, he sucked in his cheeks and pushed out his lips. He hooked his fingers like claws and took a sudden step at Mrs. Bolton. She gave a jump.

'That's enough. Keep away, Wix.'

He made a sound like a bull bellowing.

'All right, boy. That's enough.'

'And Phil can be New Zealand. He's tallest in the class.'

Mrs. Bolton looked at them. She saw that the Miller boy was half a head taller, and then, with surprise, better-looking too, if he brushed his hair. Noel Wix looked rather Italian and had a rubber face that wouldn't keep still. Miller, on the other hand . . .

'Come here, both of you.' She stood them back to back, then said to Phil, 'Show me your teeth.'

He showed them.

'Yes, all right. But you'll have to clean yourself up, boy. New Zealand doesn't have greasy hair.' She gave it a tug and wiped her fingertips on her dress. 'And nails. Just look at them. Quite filthy, Miller. Out to the tap and scrub them straight away.'

Phil went. He sent a murderous look at Noel from the door.

CHAPTER THREE

Buck's Hole

IRENE AND KITTY were no more friends than Noel and Phil, but they wanted to be. Kitty admired Irene's aloofness, and envied her skill on the piano, and her clothes, and liked her prettiness, her pink and white skin and black, shiny hair; while Irene, who was not aloof, and hated to be thought so, but was cut off from her classmates by her voice and clothes and her mother's pretensions, and was too proud to work at coming close, saw in Kitty, noisy and careless and popular, many of the things she wanted to be. It was the first year they had been in the same class. Kitty had skipped standard five (which did not please Noel). She was quick at learning — too clever by half, Mrs. Bolton thought — but it came naturally. She did not have to work very hard. Everything interested her, and what she was interested in, she remembered. She was big for her age and rather clumsy. Like Irene, she took piano lessons from Frau Stauffel, but cleverness did not help in that. She played, according to Noel, like a bunch of bananas, and the sight of Irene's fingers, skipping and dancing and sometimes seeming to stamp with a skinny ferocity on the keys, filled her with longing and admiration, and sometimes with bitter envy. She did not join in the game of making fun of Charmy-Barmy.

That lunch hour she was sitting under the trees with two of her friends, Melva Dyer and June Truelove, talking about the pageant. Melva had been chosen to play India, and June, Egypt, and they were excited about the costumes they would wear.

'I'll wear a turban with jewels in it,' Melva said.

'I'll paint my cheeks. And wear baggy trousers,' June said. 'Fancy having to be on the same side as Phil Miller.'

'He stinks,' Melva said. 'I saw a flea jump off his shirt.'

'Where did it land? Hee, here's Gallant Little Belgium. Irene, a flea jumped off Phil Miller on to your dress.'

'You'll have to dance with him in the pageant.'

'And kiss him too.'

There was something especially exciting in imagining Irene with Phil Miller. It was a game they often played. Irene took no notice. She put her lunch-basket on the grass and sat down by Kitty, leaving a gap large enough to make it seem she was by herself.

'Phil Miller likes you,' June said.

'He's got your name carved in the lid of his desk.'

'I don't care.'

'He's got a heart with initials in it,' June said.

Melva tried a new tack. 'Your mummy wouldn't like you sitting with us.'

'When are you going away to a private school, Irene?'

'I'm not.'

'Mrs. Bolton told my mother you were.'

'I'm not. I like it here.'

'You like Phil Miller. You're in love with him.'

'The flea bit him and now it's biting you.'

Irene began to feel dizzy. The words seemed to come out of the trees, and from the sky, not from Melva and June. She wanted to scream and she wanted to cry, and wanted also to go far away. She wondered how Kitty Wix could be so quiet.

'I wonder who it likes biting best.'

'Soon there'll be lots of little fleas.'

Irene closed her basket. She managed to stand up and that seemed to put her far away from Melva and June, but it did not shift her away from Kitty. Unless Kitty did something this moment was going to grow more horrible. She would never believe in kindness or goodness again.

Kitty too was faced with something simple. She liked Melva and June, but if she let them do this to Irene, she was doing it too. That made her sick. It was as though she had eaten something bad and her stomach wanted to get rid of it. So she stood up. It was difficult. Her legs felt swollen. She picked up her lunchpaper. 'Wait a minute, Irene. I'm coming too.'

Melva and June were sitting on the grass like two wooden puppets with open mouths, waiting for someone to make them talk. Kitty and Irene walked away. They found a place under a lime tree and finished their lunch.

'Did Bolters really say you were going away to a private school?'

'Probably. She's been talking to my mother. *She* wants me to.'

'Do you want to go?'

'Sometimes. With pigs like June and Melva. Mostly I like

34

it here though. I pretend I'm sick. I can make myself faint. Then dad says I've got to live at home. I can make him do most things I want.' A look of slyness made her face go gnomish. Kitty found it exciting. She saw through adults easily, but could not shake off her feeling of being ruled.

'Can you teach me to faint?'

'You hold your breath,' Irene said . . .

They sat under the lime tree, practicing, and did not hear the shouting from the back field. Clippy Hedges heard it and strode out of the staffroom and across the field and parted the yelling boys with his hands and found Noel and Phil wrestling on the grass. Phil had a leg bar on Noel and was leaning so hard that the knee bones seemed on the point of springing apart; and Noel had captured one of Phil's hands and was bending the fingers back like willow twigs. Hedges expected to hear them snap. Their faces were atrocious; they appalled him. He gave a bellow and seized them and flung them apart.

'Clear off, the lot of you!' he shouted at the spectators. Then he marched Phil and Noel into his classroom by their shirts. He strode to his table and took his strap and let it fall out to its full length.

'Who started it? Wix?'

Noel said nothing. Phil had, coming up and shouldering him, but he could not say so. All he knew was that he was sorry he hadn't let Phil be the Hun.

'Miller?'

Phil shrugged. He didn't care about getting strapped. He hoped it would make Wix howl. He didn't need help from Wix, with Bolters or anyone.

'Both gone dumb?'

'No one started it, Sir. It just happened,' Noel said.

'An act of God, eh? Like an earthquake?' Hedges laughed sourly. He rolled his strap and threw it in the drawer. Noel couldn't help giving Phil a grin.

'Yes, grin away,' Hedges said. 'But why should I be a thug just because you are? Come and see this.' He took a chart from the drawer and held it flat on the table. The boys came to his side and looked at his finger tapping the pink petals of something they took at first for a rose. 'The human brain. That's the cerebrum. That's what makes us human.' He rapped them on the head with his knuckles. 'We're supposed to think with it. And here, down here, that's the reptile brain. Left over from when we lived in the swamp. That's what you've been using. Do you want to be a man or a crocodile, Wix?'

'Yes, Sir. I'm sorry.' He thought it wasn't fair. He hadn't started the fight.

'Miller?' Phil just shrugged. He was not going to apologize.

'I've got a good mind to cut out your swimming,' Hedges said.

'You can't do that, Sir,' Noel said.

'Can't I?'

'It's our diving test.'

'I hadn't forgotten. I'll think about it. Off you go now, the pair of you. And see if you can use your brains instead of just your brawn.' But he called Phil back. 'Let me look at that knee. Put your foot on the chair.'

Phil lifted his foot and Hedges got some cotton wool and iodine from his cupboard. He looked at the bleeding scab on Phil's knee and wondered if it was impetigo, then saw it was crusted blood from a graze. He picked it off with cotton wool and dropped it in his wastepaper basket. 'This will hurt.' He dabbed iodine in the wound. Phil gave a hiss.

'Have you thought about college, Miller?' Hedges asked.

'No, Sir.' Phil spoke in a lifeless voice. He hated this subject.

'Did you ask your father?'

'He doesn't want me to go.'

'What about you?'

'I don't care.'

'Would you like me to talk to him?'

'No, Sir. Don't do that.' Phil was alive now. He did not want Hedges to find out he was living alone.

'Well, I'll see. You could do college. If you worked.'

'I want to get a job. Get some money.'

Hedges believed that. The boy needed better food and clothes — but money by itself wouldn't be enough. What he really needed was better care. His mother had died five years ago, and his brothers and sisters had been shunted off to an aunt in Christchurch. Then his father had lost his job as a tally clerk and sunk to rag-and-bone man, pushing a handcart round the streets and nipping into back alleys for a swig of gin from the bottle he kept hidden in the rags. Come to think of it, Hedges hadn't seen Charlie Miller for a month or two.

'How is your dad, anyway?'

'He's all right. He's good, Sir.'

'I haven't seen him.'

'He's been working down the other end of town.'

'Mm, I see.'

'Can I go now?'

37

'Yes, off you go.'

He watched Phil cross the playground, and heave a smaller boy out of his way. His aggressiveness came from being treated with contempt. Time was short, Hedges thought, if he was going to do anything for Phil. He grew sour about the need to make him acceptable to people who practiced such easy scorn. What he should try to do was give the boy his chance to be anything he wanted, and to hell with Jessop. Just now all he could manage was not to cancel swimming. Phil was like a fish in the water.

Hedges wouldn't have minded disappointing smug young Master Wix.

◆

At 2 o'clock standard six started for the river. They crossed the footbridge from the town and went along the clay path through the scrub to Marwick's Road. The girls went into another path leading to Girlie's Hole, where Kitty was soon in trouble with Mrs. Bolton for swimming by the rapids and swimming overarm. 'Swim like a lady, Kitty,' Mrs. Bolton called. She did not like anything more strenuous than dog-paddling. Meanwhile, the boys had crossed the one-way bridge to Marwick's farm and turned up the bank of the river towards Buck's Hole. The Marwick house stood several hundred yards off, with gables, fretwork, finials, a corner tower, white as marble against the dark-green bush. Its roof had faded to a washed-out pink, with a rusty patch here and there, but it managed to look like a fairy castle — though its denizens were anything but fairy, Hedges thought.

'Don't go in till I get there,' he shouted to the boys in the lead. 'In fact, stay with me.' He had seen Edgar Marwick shoveling dirt into a barrow in the garden.

The boys came running back. 'Sir! Sir! They've put a notice up.'

'Where?' He followed through the scrub and came to it, a good bit of workmanship, with the post skinned and dried and the board notched in, and the message itself lettered neatly: *Private Property. Keep Out. By Order, J. and E. Marwick.*

'They can't do that, can they?' Noel asked.

'No, they can't.' Hedges looked across the paddocks at Edgar Marwick, leaning on his spade now, watching them. Marwick made him nervous: a man with a burning in his eyes, a rage in him not held down properly. Hedges was sure of his position, however. He had no intention of letting this notice stand. The river holes belonged to the town. As long as the boys kept on this side of the fence, they had legal access.

'They're cheeky devils,' Hedges said. 'Pull it out. Wobble it, that's right. Now give it a lift.'

They cheered as the post came free. They tossed it like a caber down the bank into a patch of blackberries. Hedges saw Marwick striding for the house, to get new orders from his Ma, no doubt: Mrs. Julia Marwick. He'd never met her, but seen her once or twice sitting in her wicker chair on the veranda, with a floppy hat over her face and, he thought, a stick clasped in her hands. She gave an impression of witch and spider, disturbing to Hedges — although he was fond of spiders and liked the idea of witches too. It was the way she sat at the center of things he found disturbing. It seemed to give her power, and secret knowledge. The notice was her idea, no doubt about that. He wondered what she would tell her son to do.

'All right, down to the pool. Strip off. Don't go in. Wait for the reading.'

He left them pulling off their clothes and crossed the shingle bank to the water. The loveliness of this pool took his breath away. It always happened. The sand and shingle, oatmeal colored, with red pebbles, white pebbles, speckled ones and brown, strewn about like some Caliph's treasure, and the water with the clarity of air and the coldness of stone, and the mossy banks, the bush with caves of shadow, the flow in, brittle, pure, the flow out, smooth as glass, and the green deeps, with the river floor somehow warm at the bottom — it held him in a moment of delight. Then he crouched at the water and dipped in his thermometer. Warm today, warmer than last time. The trout would be feeling uncomfortable. He looked at the mercury thread. 'Sixty-eight. Everyone in.'

They ran past him, shouting, boys naked and boys togged, with brown backs and white behinds, with grazed knees and stubbed toes and knobbly elbows and knobbly spines. They went in with a flurry of water and a chorus of screeches, and reduced his pleasure in the pool not at all. The place belonged to them. Soon it would go back to its quietness. He let them horseplay for ten minutes. Then he called the non-swimmers and made them lie on the shingle practicing strokes. He climbed along the bank to the deep part of the pool and called Miller and Wix for their diving test. They came along like monkeys, one in bright-red togs, the other in a pair thrown out in a rag-bag, with ravelled holes in the wool and a leather bootlace for a belt.

'Who's first? You're not going to quarrel about that too?'

'He can go,' Noel said.

Hedges took a tin lid from his pocket and flicked it into the water. It fluttered like a leaf going down, and shone like the belly of a fish.

'All right, Miller. If you get short of breath come up quick.'

Phil made a clean dive. He knew there had been no splash, just a boiling on the surface. He grinned going down — let Wix do better — and swam fast in water full of sun. It was as easy as walking. There was a glare above him like a sky, and the pebble bottom leading on, and a brown trout under the bank, safe and still. He felt easy, strong, in control. Bubbles of air swelled at his lips, tickling them. He felt like yelling out, and not going back, though going back with the lid and waving it was a kind of treasure he saved up. His hands seemed very white. The bottom slanted down. And there, far away, looking bent, was the cigarette lid. It winked like an eye. He went towards it, digging in the sand, sending up puffs of silt like a crayfish. He grabbed the lid and put it in his teeth, thinking of pirates. It almost made him lose his air and he shot a look at the surface, making sure. It stretched like a cloth made of silk. Leaves lay flat on it and shadows loomed and shrank. That must be the bush. Hedges, up there, would be getting worried. He was probably timing things with his watch. Phil wished there was a record for staying down. He could go a while yet, even though his chest was getting sore. Then he glimpsed something deeper down. It was green and yellow and seemed to make a word, but he could not read it. He made a stroke towards it. The lid seemed to shift in his teeth and he took it out and knew he had no more time. With a beating of feet and a grabbing of hands, he made for the surface.

'You took your time. Did you meet a mermaid down there?' Hedges said. He leaned out for the lid and Phil swam to him and held it up.

'Right ho, Wix.'

Noel's dive was a good one too, just a bit of bending in his legs. Hedges got a splash on his trousers that made Phil grin. When he'd got his breath he put his face in the water and watched Noel going into the deep part of the pool, away from him. He thought he saw the lid winking there, but could not see the green and yellow thing. Noel angled down, as short as a dwarf, with the white soles of his feet waving like hands. A stream of silver bubbles came round the side of his neck. He seemed to have trouble getting deep enough and Phil hoped he wasn't going to make it. But he made a grab, and had the lid, and kicked straight for the surface. Phil swam out to meet him.

'Did you see that thing down there?'

'Saw something. What was it?'

'Don't know,' Phil said. 'It had words on it.'

'A good effort, Wix,' Hedges called. 'Let me have that lid. Then get down the shallow end and practice your breast-stroke.'

'Sir, I'm cold,' a boy called from the bank.

'All right, get dressed. Anyone else who's cold get dressed.'

Noel and Phil swam to the shallow end. 'It must be twenty feet,' Noel said.

'We could get it. Unless you're scared.'

'I'm not scared.'

42

Phil saw he was. It made him feel good. 'We'll come back after school.'

'Sir! Sir!' The boy came running from the scrub. 'Someone's taken our clothes.'

'Nonsense, boy,' Hedges said. He came along the bank and crossed the shingle. Boys crowded round him. 'It's true, Sir. They're all gone.' He strode into the clearing where the boys undressed. Half a dozen towels lay on the grass, that was all.

'All right, who was it?'

'It wasn't us, Sir, honest.'

'It's a good joke but we're getting cold.'

'We were all in the water, Sir.'

Phil had crossed the clearing. 'Sir,' he called, 'there's a shirt over here.' It was caught on a gorse bush. 'There's a shoe by the fence.'

Hedges broke through the bushes and picked it up. He looked over the paddocks at the house. Edgar Marwick was on the veranda, leaning on a post. He seemed to be rolling a cigarette.

'It must have been him, Sir,' Noel said.

'No doubt of it,' Hedges said. He bit his lip.

'What are you going to do, Sir?'

Hedges thought for a moment. 'Pay him a visit. All of us.'

'We could strip him, Sir. Until he gives ours back.'

'No, mustn't touch him. See that shed by the house. Wait behind it until I call. How many without any togs? Eight of you. You're my savages. Off we go. Use the gate. Don't climb his fence.'

They went through the gate and walked up the paddock, the naked boys shivering and covering their loins. Fifty yards short of the house, Hedges waved them off towards the shed. He saw Edgar Marwick speak to someone in the house, over his shoulder. Hedges let himself through a gate on to a croquet lawn unused for years. Rusty hoops stood in tufts of grass. Marwick was more the type for bare-knuckle boxing. He had thick hairy arms and hairy wrists and shoulders that strained against his shirt. His green eyes seemed to smoulder. Smoke from his cigarette slid over his face and broke in his hair. A good-looking man in his way, though lumpy in his nose and jaw. He was like boys Hedges had known: sulky, disappointed, damaged in ways that could not be repaired.

'He's here, Ma,' Marwick said.

Mrs. Marwick came on to the veranda. She was a tall old lady, elegant. Her floppy-brimmed straw hat had a silk rose in the band. But Hedges saw how ravaged her stateliness was. Her eyes blinked against the sudden light. Her skin was powdered white and a little rain of powder had fallen on the embroidered purple of her jacket. She was like an ancient lizard coming into the sun. She prodded with her black stick, as though keeping things away.

Hedges took off his hat. 'Mrs. Marwick.'

'What do you want here?' Her voice had bell-tones, startling: a clear musical voice from her old mouth.

'You're trespassing, schoolteacher,' Marwick said.

Hedges was glad to turn from his mother to him. 'I came for what was stolen, Mr. Marwick.'

Marwick flicked cigarette ash away. 'What was that?'

'My boys' clothes. I'll have them back.'

'Who says I took them?'

But Mrs. Marwick slapped her stick against his trouser

leg. 'It's all right, Edgar, I'll deal with it. You, Mr. Schoolteacher what's-your-name? We have the clothes. And we'll keep them until I have your promise that you'll keep your rabble of town boys off my land. I want my notice put back, too.'

'No, Mrs. Marwick.'

'How dare you say no?'

'There's legal access to the river.'

'I don't recognize it. This land has been mine for fifty years.'

'But not the river. The court awarded access. The pools are vested in the town.'

She made little jabs at him with her stick and he stepped back. She'd poke his eyes out. 'Courts? Courts? They've nothing to do with me. Stay off my land. Or you and your riff-raff can slink home through the bushes.'

Hedges smiled. He liked a fight. He had lost his sense that this was a lady to be in awe of. 'There won't be any slinking, Mrs. Marwick.' He turned and called, 'Boys! Come up here.'

They ran from behind the shed and across the paddock. They let themselves on to the croquet lawn. Hedges beckoned them. 'Closer. Right up here. These are the people who stole your clothes. Say good afternoon.'

'Good afternoon, Mrs. Marwick. Good afternoon, Mr. Marwick,' said the boys. The naked ones stayed at the back, shielding themselves, but Marwick glimpsed them. He threw down his cigarette. It seemed he would jump from the veranda. Mrs. Marwick closed her stick in front of him like a gate.

'I've seen naked children before,' she said to Hedges.

'Where's my savages? Where's my warrior boys? Come out. Do a dance for Mrs. Marwick.'

The eight came to the front, some ashamed but others bold as brass. They began leaping up and down, flinging their skinny limbs and howling at the sky in a primitive dance. The boys in togs took up the chant, raising their faces.

'Walla walla walla! Eee! Eee!' they cried.

'Stop that. Stop that noise,' Mrs. Marwick cried.

'When we have our clothes.'

'Chase them away, Edgar.'

He jumped down from the veranda, but Phil put out his leg and tripped him. He sprawled on his face. Boys piled on him and held him down, two or three on each limb and Phil kneeling on his back. Noel climbed on to the veranda. He meant to search the house, but Hedges called sharply, 'Don't go in. Now, Mrs. Marwick, we'll stop when we have our clothes.'

'There, there, there,' the old lady cried, jabbing with her stick, and in the end whacking Noel on his legs. He went where she had pointed and found a coal sack stuffed behind some boxes.

'Here, Sir.' He hauled it out and flung it down to Hedges.

'All right, boys, that's enough!' Hedges yelled. 'Off behind the shed. Get dressed.'

They ran off in a yelling mob, carrying the sack over their heads.

Marwick climbed to his feet. He was panting like a dog. 'You'll pay for this, Hedges. I'm getting the police.'

'Then I'll charge you with theft, Mr. Marwick. I have

thirty witnesses.' He waved at the shed, where the last of the boys ran from sight.

The old lady on the veranda said nothing. She turned and went into the house without a glance at him or her son. Her stick tapped down a hall. Hedges felt he had seen the ancient lizard withdraw. His sense of fear returned. She seemed to have come out for a look at the world and returned to the dark where she lived. He was happier facing her son. His sort of anger he could manage. He put his hat on, nodded at the man, and walked away. He took the boys down the paddock, through the gate, along past the pool. He began to feel pleased with himself, and liked the excitement of the boys. Soon he began to sing, 'Men of Harlech, wake from sleeping . . .' and they took it up. He felt like the leader of a tribe.

Phil and Noel slipped off into the scrub and crept along the riverbank to Buck's Hole.

CHAPTER FOUR

Clippy Pays a Call

THEY DIVED in at the deepest part. Noel wasn't sure he could reach the bottom, but as he went down side by side with Phil, he found himself level. The bottom shelved away from the place where the lid had been. A rib of stone curved up from the shingle with a rotten log across the top of it, putting out legs. The green and yellow object lay in the hollow, half buried in silt which sprang up like smoke at their touch. 'Tor', they read, but did not stay to puzzle it out. The thing was a can, that much was plain, and Phil seized the handle and kicked for the surface. Noel put his hand under it. A can, with holes chopped in it. By the time they reached the surface he had managed to read the name. 'Motor spirit,' he shouted as they broke into the air.

'Yeah,' Phil said. 'Get it on the bank.'

They climbed on to a ledge but had to let the water pour out the holes before they could lift the can up.

'He really made sure of sinking it.'

'Who?'

'The fire-raiser. Fire-bug. He uses benzine. Motor spirit. They found an empty can in Dargie's.'

'We better get it back in the bush, eh?'

They carried the can into the scrub. Then they got their clothes and dressed. Cicadas were scraping all around but it seemed deathly silent.

'Let's get out. In case he comes. I've got to get to work, anyway.'

They hid the can in some bracken and crept away. On the road to town they ran side by side, and then single file along the paths at the foot of Settlers Hill. They crossed the river on the railway bridge, hugging piles as a train rumbled over. Noel was out of his territory. He let Phil lead, and when they came to Chalmers' seed and grain warehouse, he stayed to talk with him while he worked. Phil's job was cleaning the yard. He shovelled horse dung into a barrow and transferred it to a cart at the gates, then he hosed down the cobbles. It wasn't a job Noel thought much of, but he admired the way Phil yelled at the draymen, telling them not to let their horses muck up his yard.

Phil leaned on his shovel. 'So? What are we going to do?'

'Tell the police.'

'They wouldn't believe. You maybe. Not me.'

'What about Clippy?'

'He'd tell us off for going back.'

Noel wasn't worried about that, but felt he had to back Phil up. He also had to show he wasn't scared. 'We could set up a watch at the pool. Me half the night, you the other.' It was the last thing he wanted to do.

'Nah,' Phil said. 'It could be weeks before he came. If he ever does. That was a five-gallon can. Take ages to use all that. Even if he burns the cathedral down.'

Noel was relieved. 'I reckon it's Marwick.'

'I reckon it's his mother.'

49

They laughed, and felt easier with each other, and Noel went up the street and bought some licorice from a shop. They ate it in the yard while Phil hosed down.

◆

Mrs. Bolton marched her girls back from the river, but let them break up after crossing the footbridge. Kitty's hair was plastered to her neck. Swimming underwater was forbidden — unladylike, like most things in Mrs. Bolton's world — but she'd managed to fall in off the bank and nothing could be done about that. Drops of water trickled down her back. She asked Irene to dry it.

'I wish we could swim nuddy, like the boys,' Irene said.

'With old Bolters? What would she be like with nothing on?'

That was a daring thing for Kitty to say, quite unlike her, and she wondered what her mother would think about it. Irene laughed.

'Like a huhu grub.'

'Like my dad's bread before he bakes it.' That was enough. Bringing her father in wasn't right. She said, 'I've got music. I've got to hurry.'

'Can I come for a minute? I like Frau Stauffel.'

'As long as you don't listen to me play,' Kitty said.

They walked past the school to the Wix house and Kitty ran in for her music. Then they went down the street to Frau Stauffel's, a cottage with a green roof in a nest of oleander trees. A brass plate by the door said: 'Lotte Stauffel, Pianoforte.' What a lot it didn't say, Irene thought. It didn't say she was kind and made you happy. Or that she was sad, and missing her young husband, dead twenty years — 'killed on a foolish mountain that he must reach the top of' — and missing her own country. Or that she played like seven angels (as Clippy Hedges said). Pianoforte sounded so proper, but Frau Stauffel could make storms, thunder and lightning, and oceans, and waterfalls, and singing birds, all those things, trees, flowers, cats and mice, wind and water. As well as that, she could do what Irene called 'piano sums'. She could put things together, take them apart, go from one to another by invisible bridges, invisible numbers, and arrive at the one place in the end. Irene did not know whether that was science or magic. All she knew was that she must learn to do it herself.

Kitty knocked at the door. Feet came down the hall, and there she was: lovely plump Frau Stauffel, with apple cheeks and pixie chin, blue-china eyes, and a mouth like pink icing smoothed with a knife. Now that pretty mouth fell open.

'Oh, Irenee!'

'She came to say hello, Frau Stauffel, but she's not allowed to listen,' Kitty said.

'Irenee. Irenee.'

'What's the matter?'

'Come in. Quickly.' She drew them in and closed the door.

'I'm only here for a minute,' Irene said. 'Kitty won't play otherwise. I've done the Handel. I've got it perfectly. I'll show you tomorrow.'

'Tomorrow? Oh, Irenee!' Tears rolled on Frau Stauffel's cheeks.

Kitty gaped, but Irene stepped forward, sharp as a knife. Her fingers fastened on Frau Stauffel's wrist. 'What's gone wrong?'

'I have a letter from your mother.'

'Yes?'

'She is taking you away. I cannot teach you any more.'

'She can't do that!'

'It is done. I am paid off.'

'Why?'

'Because I am German. She does not say, but that is it.'

'German?'

'Because of the war. I am Hun.'

'You are not. And it doesn't matter.'

'Today it matters. People throw stones on my roof. They put filthy things in my letterbox. But I am not important. Oh, Irenee, you *must* play.'

To Kitty it seemed that Irene had shrunk. She looked like a little dry gnome, like Rumpelstiltskin. She was white as flour, but two little patches of red stood like a fever rash on her cheeks. Her lips were crumpled like paper. Then she stamped. She made a movement with her hands as though tearing something in pieces.

'I won't let her,' she whispered. 'She takes everything away from me.'

'What can you do, my child? She is your mother.'

Kitty jumped forward. 'She can have my lessons. We can come together and she can play instead of me.'

'No,' Frau Stauffel said. 'It is falsehood. It is thieving. And will not work.'

'Does my father know?' Irene said.

'The letter was from her. Mrs. Anne Chalmers.'

Irene straightened up. Her eyes blinked as she worked something out. 'I'll go and see my father. I'll make him do something.'

'Ah Irenee, he is weak vessel. He cannot change her.'

'We'll see.'

'You must practice hard at home. You must work hard for your new teacher.'

'I don't want a new teacher. Kitty, come on. You can tell him your mother and father let you come to Frau Stauffel.'

'What about my lesson?'

'You can miss. You're no good at it anyhow.'

◆

Thomas Hedges was in a mood to get things done. His victory over the Marwicks had set him bubbling with energy and he saw no reason why Mrs. Chalmers should not be brought into line. Everything about her house seemed to challenge him: the neat flowerbeds, the summerhouse, the path with its raked red scoria, shipped at huge cost from Auckland, the sugar-cake fretwork, the corner tower, the discreet sign directing tradesmen to the back, and the name, 'Hollyhurst', lettered in glass by the door. Didn't these people know they lived in a rough little land at the end of the world, where Christmas came in summer and no man had a master? It angered him that one of his bright girls of five years ago should answer the door, dressed in a maid's white apron and cap.

'Ah, Nancy.' He grinned and lowered his voice. 'Not broken any more vases, I hope?'

The girl looked quickly over her shoulder. 'No, Mr. Hedges, but I spilled a glass of water on her last night.'

'Spill the soup next time. There are better jobs. Any chance of seeing her?'

But when he was in the parlor facing Mrs. Chalmers, he felt less confident. It was a foreign country. He could not speak the language. To that English lady in her chair — that

53

lady being English in her chair — he was a tradesman. Well, he thought grimly, it's no bad thing. I'm the one who's got a job to do. And he told her how gifted her daughter was; that in all his years of teaching he had not known any child with a greater feeling for music or better skills — and that being the case, she must have the very best teaching available. That meant, of course, Frau Stauffel, who had studied in Vienna, and had been a pupil of Hauss, who had been a pupil of Liszt. The line of tuition came down from the greatest pianist of his century.

Mrs. Chalmers made well-bred faces at the names. 'There are things more important, Mr. Hedges. But, confining it to music, Irene shows excessive enthusiasm and I don't care for it.'

'She doesn't feel it's excessive.'

'What she feels has no bearing on it. We feel — Mr. Chalmers and I — that Irene has had all the music she requires. Moderation, we feel, is more important at this point. Much of what she played seemed so noisy. And it's not as if she needs music as a livelihood, unlike Frau Stauffel. As a matter of fact, Mr. Hedges, I'm pleased to have the instrument out of the house.' She saw that Hedges did not understand. 'I had some men take the piano away. It seemed the patriotic thing to do.'

'Patriotic?'

'It was a German one.'

'But,' Hedges said, and could say no more. He could not have been more appalled if she had told him Irene was to be kept on bread and water. However, he mastered himself and said dryly, 'I hope you didn't keep the money.'

'As a matter of fact, I donated it to the Belgian Relief Fund.' She picked up a little hand-bell engraved with forget-me-nots and tinkled it once. Nancy came in, and Mrs. Chalmers said, 'Show Mr. Hedges out. And Mr. Hedges, another word. Irene will be going to a private school very soon. Mr. Chalmers will be in touch with you. Good day.'

He went out into the sunshine and felt he had come out of prison. A thrush was singing in a walnut tree, but that did not bother him. The bird had settled down here, unlike the woman in the house. England was ten thousand miles away, and English gardens, and the song it sang was a New Zealand one. Mrs. Chalmers, playing ladies, was a foreigner — more foreign, he thought, than Lotte Stauffel. Unfortunately though, she could damage people.

He walked down from nob hill into the town, meaning to have a word with Chalmers, but when he reached the Council Chambers he saw Irene going in with Kitty Wix, and the girl had such a fierce look on her face he guessed she knew what had happened and was all set to do something about it. Best leave it to her. She was a tough little thing and no doubt could twist her father round. He felt sorry for the man, caught between self-important wife and strong-minded daughter, and walked on, grinning. He crossed the park and went along by the tidal stretch of the river, through the poorer part of the port settlement, and came out by the warehouses and wharves. This was his day for tackling problems. He was on his way to see Charlie Miller.

◆

His Worship the Mayor, Francis Chalmers, was feeling groggy, and feeling mean, and feeling resentful — all by turns. He was conscious of his importance and couldn't understand how his twelve-year-old daughter could reduce him to this state. Looking at her shrewish face, with

55

snapping eyes and snapping mouth, over his desk, he found himself wondering where this fierce person lived, who she was, and what her relationship could be with the Irene who sat so quietly on the sofa at home. He knew he should be able to stop all this by raising his finger, looking stern, but she had a spell on him. He was paralyzed. He was frightened, too, of what would happen when she found out what else her mother had done.

'Now Irene, you know how she is when she makes up her mind. There's no chance of going back to Frau Stauffel.'

'Pa — '

'Find something else, eh? Tell you what, I'll buy you a kitten.'

'I don't want a kitten. I'll drown it in the river.'

Kitty Wix spoke up. 'I go to Frau Stauffel. My mother says she's the best teacher in town.'

'I'd sooner have a new mother than a new teacher,' Irene said.

'Now you don't mean that, dear.'

'I'll run away from home. I'll live with Frau Stauffel."

Chalmers looked at her desperately. 'A pony? And a saddle? A piebald pony?'

'I hate horses.'

'But Frau Stauffel,' Chalmers cried, 'she's a German. And the piano . . .' He hadn't meant to say it, but it was out. Quickly he added, 'It's her doing, not mine.'

'Yes? What?' Now she had changed again. She was cold and dangerous. She was an adult.

Woefully Chalmers said, 'She sold the piano.'

'Sold it! My piano!'

'We'll buy another one. An English one.'

'I don't want an English one. I want mine.'

'Don't, love. Please don't make a fuss.' He was so pa-thetic, Kitty felt like going and holding his hand. He took off his glasses and wiped the skin round his eyes. She had never seen anyone look so naked or helpless. 'She'll send you away to school.'

'If I don't get my piano back I'll *go* away to school,' Irene answered. To Kitty it seemed she had grown up fifteen years. It made her shiver. She saw how little she knew Irene Chalmers.

A gentle little knocking came on the door, a secretary knock, and the man put his head in and coughed. That gave Francis Chalmers a chance to grow back to his full height. 'Yes. What is it?'

'Mr. Marwick wants to see you, Sir. He's very insistent.'

'Tell him to wait.'

'I don't think he'll do that, Sir.'

The door was pushed in roughly and the secretary hauled aside. Edgar Marwick stood there, hands on hips, chin thrust out. 'I want to talk to you, Chalmers.'

'You'll wait,' Chalmers said. 'You'll go back there and sit on a chair and wait your turn. Or else I'll call a policeman and have you removed.'

'You listen — '

'At once! Do as I say.'

Edgar Marwick blinked. He took his hands off his hips. 'All right,' he growled, 'but I haven't got much time. So shake a leg.' He turned and went back to the outer office and the secretary leaned in and closed the door.

Chalmers kept himself puffed up. He faced his daughter and frowned. 'All right, young lady, I'll think about your problems. Off you go.'

'Daddy, I want my piano.'

'Don't speak to me in that voice, Miss. I'll do what I can. Now, I've got business, as you can see. Here's a shilling. Buy a bottle of fizz. Two bottles.' He gave Irene the coin. 'Don't drink them in the street. Come back here.'

He shunted them out. Irene did not argue. She saw that she had done as much as she could, but she gave a cross look at the angry man, Marwick, as she went through the outer room. He had come and spoiled it just when her father was curling up.

◆

Hedges pulled a face as he looked at the Miller house. It stood in a narrow street at the back of wharf sheds, the only occupied one in a line of derelict shanties. Fitter for rats than humans, he thought. The boards were rotten, broken away from the framing, the roof had patches of rust and dents as though a giant had punched it with his fist. The door, half open, was jammed on the floor, where it had worn a shiny, sickle-shaped groove. Charlie Miller's empty handcart stood in a yard littered with cans and bricks and warped boards and bottles with yellow water and fungus in them. Hedges rolled them aside with his shoe. He knocked at the door. 'Charlie?'

No answer came. He knocked again and called more loudly, then stepped inside. After the bright day, the room was as dark as a cave. It was furnished with two chairs and a table, one of whose legs had a fence paling tied on it as a splint. Two plates and two cups stood on a shelf, and a pot and pan were on a wood range let into the wall. A torn shirt was drying on a wire rack by the chimney. Nothing covered the floor but grit and dust balls. But someone had made an effort to tidy the place. A tear in the curtain was sewn up with string. The table had a newspaper spread on it as a cloth. 'British Forces Take Neuve Chapelle', Hedges read, and he gave a snort of amusement. That showed a retentive mind, at least.

'Miller,' he called. He looked in a half-curtained alcove where a mattress lay on the floor with a blanket on it. He sniffed, expecting the place to reek of gin, but only picked up whiffs of grease and cabbage. Then he saw a sheet of paper spiked on a nail, and peered in the dim light and made out Halley's Comet, long-tailed on a black sky. So, he thought, the little devil — but he was pleased.

Phil burst in. He came so fast he crashed into the door and sent it shrieking back two feet in its groove on the floor. He faced Hedges, panting.

'What do you want?'

'Ah, Phil.' Hedges stepped out of the alcove. 'I thought I'd have a word with your father.'

'What for? You've got no right coming in here.'

Thomas Hedges was not used to being told by boys what he could do, but he kept his temper. He crossed the room and sat in a chair, which threatened to tip him off, it was so wobbly. 'Where did you spring from?' he asked Phil.

'At my job. I saw you down the street.'

'Job, eh?'

'I clean the yard at Chalmers'.'

'Pay you much?'

'Sixpence.'

'The skinflint! I'll have a word with him.'

'No!' Hedges raised his eyebrows. 'It's *my* job. I can look after myself.'

'So you say.' He looked around. 'Only one mattress. Where does your father sleep?'

'We share it.'

'I see. And who does the cooking? And who does the housework?'

'I do.' Phil came further into the room. 'It's tidier than this most of the time.'

'Yes, I see. I'm more worried about your education. Where is he?'

Phil looked down sullenly. 'Work,' he said.

'His cart's in the yard.'

'He doesn't do that any more.'

'A proper job, eh?'

'Yes,' Phil said.

'Does that mean he's stopped drinking?'

'Yes. He has.'

'Good for him. Where's he working?'

Phil shrugged. He turned to Noel, standing in the door. 'Get out, Wix. I didn't ask you in.'

Hedges saw the diversion. 'Where, Miller?'

'None of your business.'

Hedges banged the table with his hand. 'Answer me!'

'In the mill,' Phil muttered.

'What, White's Landing? Over the hill? So you're living alone?'

'He sends me money. I can look after myself. I can cook stew. And cabbage. Potatoes.'

'I'm sure you can. But you can't live alone, boy. And you can't do yourself justice at school. It's getting something into your head I'm worried about.' He thought he saw a smirk on the Wix boy's face. 'What's the matter, Wix? You think because he needs a bath he's got no brains?'

'I didn't say anything.'

'He's just as brainy as you. He's almost as brainy as your sister.'

Noel said nothing and Hedges looked at him sideways. The boy was sulking. 'What are you doing down here, anyway?'

'I was helping Phil.'

'I didn't know you were friends. You were trying to break each other's necks today.'

Noel shrugged. He wasn't Phil's friend, but knew he couldn't say it.

Hedges watched them both — both of them sulking. He was amused, but had some affection for them, and a good deal of concern for Phil.

'And where did you get to today? Sneaking off after swimming?'

'Nowhere, sir.'

'No such place, boy.'

'Just another swim.'

'You didn't ask me, did you?'

They didn't reply, and Hedges sighed. He knew he'd lost his chance of getting anywhere with Phil. 'Well,' he said, standing up, 'don't do it again. You drown and your parents will see me in prison. Come on now, the pair of you. Up the road and I'll shout you a bottle of fizz. And Phil, I'll tell you the secret of a stew, handed down from my Ma. Follow me.'

He knew Phil did not get many treats.

◆

Edgar Marwick was getting nowhere with Chalmers. He remembered those prancing boys and felt their knees digging in his spine, and saw Hedges looking down at him, and he swelled with rage at the shame and insult. But Chalmers said, 'It's no good shouting. The court made its decision and I couldn't change it even if I wanted. The river pools are vested in the city.'

'You listen to me — '

'No, you listen. The public have access to the river. You can't put up a notice. If you do you're breaking the law and we'll call the police.' Chalmers laid his hands on his desk to demonstrate the end of the argument.

'That's it? That's all you've got to say?'

'It is.'

Marwick looked at him with hatred. A little pink and white plump man with fat hands and a fat little voice, he stood for the town. Marwick wanted to smash him, open the case where his chain was hanging and throttle him with it. He leaned across the desk and was pleased to see Chalmers draw back. 'You can think it's finished if you like, but I'm not finished. There's plenty of things I can do.' He turned and went to the door, and stopped and pointed his finger, felt he had Chalmers speared on it. 'You'll find out.' He strode out through the secretary's office, thumped the door open with his fist, and went down the granite steps two at a time to the street.

Kitty and Irene were coming up with bottles of raspberryade. They saw the fierce-eyed man charging at them, and tried to jump aside. Kitty was slow. He walked straight through her, striking her midriff with his hip. She went flying back across the footpath. Her bottle made a neat double arc and smashed at her feet as she plumped down. Raspberryade ran fizzing in the dust. Edgar Marwick turned and snarled at her. Then he went on in his broken gait, half gallop, half wolfish padding, with his right arm raised like a club. Kitty, dizzy with the blow, seemed for a moment to be sitting in the gas-lit street outside the bakery. The time between had gone, and the man charging away seemed to have a black coat flapping round him and a ball of fire on his head. Irene ran to help her.

'That's him,' Kitty whispered. 'That's the man who knocked me down before.'

CHAPTER FIVE

The Letter

SHE TOLD NO ONE. Irene thought she should tell Mr. Wix, but when Kitty said, 'Would you tell your father?' agreed that parents were unlikely to believe. Kitty, though she classed her father as much superior to Mr. Chalmers, knew that adults wanted evidence and wouldn't be satisfied with just a feeling, with a flash of knowledge — for that was what it was, and though it stayed with her, she saw it would convince no one else. Irene was convinced, but she had been there, and seen the man charge off and had felt something like that flash of knowledge herself. And Irene was her friend. They understood each other, and liked each other, and felt intensely loyal, and did not think it strange that all this had come about in less than a day.

Irene asked her mother if Kitty could stay the following night. Mrs. Chalmers agreed, for it got them off the subject of pianos. She said she would drop a note to Mrs. Wix in the morning. The girls sat together under the lime trees next day and exchanged sandwiches. Irene said her father had promised her a Broadwood, but not another Bechstein,

and not her old one back, and no more lessons with Frau
Stauffel. 'But I'll go back, you wait and see.'

'Did you faint last night?'

'I'm saving that up.'

'You'd better do it now. Here comes Bolters.'

'Irene, Kitty,' Mrs. Bolton cried, 'you're late for rehearsal.
I don't expect this sort of behavior from you, Irene.'

'We were practicing our lines, Mrs. Bolton.'

'Oh, that's different. I'm glad you're setting an example.'

Meanwhile, Phil was in Hedges' room, looking at a star
chart spread on the table. He had been sour at first to be
called in from the playground, but had to admit the chart
was interesting.

'There,' Hedges said, 'the Southern Cross. This is the Al-
pha star, this is the Beta. Those are Greek words meaning
first and second. All the constellations are numbered in that
way, from the brightest star down. These,' he touched
them, 'are first magnitude stars.'

'What does that mean?'

'They're in the class of brightest stars.'

'What are constellations?'

'Groups of stars. See, here.' He pointed them out.

'Have they all got names?'

'Yes. Greek names. And individual stars have got names
too, the brightest ones. Comets, now, they're named after
the people who see them first. Halley's Comet. You've got a
picture of that, haven't you? — torn from one of my
magazines.'

'Yes, Sir.' Phil wondered if he'd been called in for punish-
ment, but Hedges seemed calm enough about it. 'I only
took it because I remember.'

'You'd only have been about six.'

'I still remember. I sat on the roof and watched it with Dad one night.'

'Ha! Good!' Hedges was pleased the boy had memories of that sort. 'I watched Halley's Comet through the observatory telescope. Made some notes for the Institute.'

'Can I look through the telescope?'

Hedges grinned. He was getting somewhere. 'You take this chart. Memorize those constellations. Then we'll see.'

Suddenly Mrs. Bolton filled the door. 'Mr. Hedges! I need this boy for rehearsals. We've lost a quarter of an hour. Miller, this is not good enough. I've a good mind to replace you.'

Hedges sighed. 'My fault, Mrs. Bolton, don't blame him. Off you go, Phil. I'll leave this chart in my drawer. Take it when you want it.' He watched out the classroom window as Mrs. Bolton led Phil over the grass to the rest of the cast under the trees. She held a corner of his shirt between thumb and forefinger, making it plain he was in disgrace and that he was a grubby thing too, not to be touched. Hedges snapped his teeth. Sooner or later something would have to be done about Mrs. Bolton.

The rehearsal was a read-through, but Noel had brought along a Prussian helmet with a spike on top and Mrs. Bolton had given Kitty the school flag to drape on her shoulders. Some of the boys had wooden rifles.

'Might is right,' Noel declaimed. 'Power is my reward. I trample through the green fields of France. I tear this poppy Belgium from her stem. My heel shall grind her petals in the mud.' He screwed his foot in the grass, grinning fiercely.

'O Britannia, Britannia, pity our distress!' Irene cried to Kitty. 'The imperious Kaiser marches his German horde across our plains to carry death.'

'Bugles!' cried Mrs. Bolton. 'Tara, tara! Drums!' she cried, beating her plump fists up and down. 'Britannia, speak!'

Kitty was tangled in her flag. She jerked it free, kicking out her feet, and said, 'Poor little Belgium, brave but powerless against the foe. Shall she be trampled underfoot while we stand by neglectful of our pledge? Fight we must and fight we will. Who will follow? Sons and daughters, speak!'

'I will follow,' the boy who was Canada cried.

'I.' Australia.

'And I.' India, Melva Dyer.

'Step forward when you say it. Be bold,' Mrs. Bolton said.

'And I,' said Egypt, June Truelove.

'Good! Good!'

Phil stepped forward. 'And I.'

'Louder, boy! New Zealand is loudest.'

'And I.' Phil faced Kitty. He held his paper by his face and read, 'Mother of Empire! Our New Zealand home is so far from the white cliffs of Old England — '

'No, Miller, no. Round vowels. Whait cliffs, whait. Say it.'

'White.' Phil said, but still it sounded 'whoit'.

'Whait,' Mrs. Bolton cried. 'You sound like a navvy, boy.'

Noel said, 'Mr. Hedges reckons New Zealanders should talk like New Zealanders and not be little mock-Englishmen.'

'Well, fortunately Mr. Hedges is not in charge of this

pageant. Irene! Where you are, Irene! Say it, dear. Whait! Show him.'

Irene, red-faced, caught off guard, said in a small voice, 'White cliffs.'

'There,' Mrs. Bolton said, 'do you hear that, Miller? That is the true English sound. Now try harder, boy . . .'

◆

'Here comes Charmy-Barmy. White, skite,' Phil said. 'You sound like a cow with bloat, Chalmers.'

'Moo-oo,' Noel joined in.

They were on the footbridge over the river, throwing in sticks and shelling them with pebbles. Irene and Kitty came along from the town side of the river.

'It's not her fault,' Kitty said.

'I don't ask her to make me pet,' Irene said. She struck a pose. 'Bugles! Tara, tara. Drums, ratatat-tat. Bolters, speak! Our New Zealand home is so far from the whait cliffs of old England . . .'

The boys grinned. Irene, without thinking, went on, 'We know who the fire-raiser is.'

'Who?' the boys said, pushing their heads at her.

Irene blinked. She didn't know how it had got out, and she said lamely, 'Kitty knows.'

'Who?'

'Someone,' Kitty said.

'Of course it's someone, dummy.'

'You don't know anything,' Phil said. 'We know. It's Marwick.'

'We've got proof,' Noel said.

'What proof?'

'A motor spirits can. Sunk in Buck's Hole.'

'Kitty saw him,' Irene said.

'Marwick?'

'He knocked me over again. Outside Mr. Chalmers' office.' The boys stared at her, unbelieving. 'He ran the same way. And held his arm up.'

'You call that proof? We found a can sunk in his pool. By his house.'

'You didn't see him put it there. Anyone could have put it there.'

'It's better than a bloke who runs with his arm stuck up.' Phil threw a pebble at a stick in the weeds and scored a hit. It made him feel good. 'Go home and practice talking, Chalmers. You might learn to say proons.'

Irene went red. 'You stink. Go and have a bath. Go and put some flea-powder on.' She jumped back as Phil lunged at her, and Kitty took her arm and pulled her away. They ran off the bridge, leaving the boys, and ran up Leckie's Lane and along past the school to Kitty's house. Mrs. Wix gave them milk and pikelets. Then she asked Irene to play the piano.

Still cross, Irene sat down and raced through *The Harmonious Blacksmith* — the Handel she had learned for Frau Stauffel. She did not enjoy it, but soon began to like showing off. Kitty and Mrs. Wix clapped when she finished. She began to be ashamed. Music was not for skiting with. So she played a Chopin nocturne, and felt sadness welling up in her, and kept control of it with her fingers, and felt almost happy when it was done.

'Oh,' Kitty sighed, 'that was wonderful.'

'Why can't you play like that, Kitty?' Mrs. Wix said.

Irene said, 'Your piano needs tuning, Mrs. Wix.'

'Oh, does it?' Mrs. Wix wasn't pleased.

Irene played a note to demonstrate. 'Uugh.' She shivered. It almost hurt her. 'It's not a very good piano, really.'

'Well, we shall have to get a new one,' Mrs. Wix said. 'I've got your stuff ready,' she said to Kitty. 'You mind your manners up there. We can't have them thinking you don't know a fork from a spoon.'

◆

Noel and Phil had decided to tell Mr. Wix about the can. There were pies to be made for White's Landing that night and Mr. Wix was surprised at the boy his son brought along to help. He made him have a soapy wash, no nonsense, and put him in an apron. Cleanliness in the bakehouse was his first rule. But he found the boy eager to help, and started to like him. He let him dust the work-bench with flour. They rolled the pastry and lined the trays and Wix hopped along with a basin, putting in steak and kidney.

'What calls back the past like a rich pumpkin pie?'

Phil was puzzled. 'This isn't pumpkin, Mr. Wix.' He pointed at a pie. 'That one's short.'

'Can't have that.' He topped it up. 'Like to be a baker, Phil?'

'If I could eat what I baked.'

'The tragedy of bakers is that they all have dyspepsia.' He seized the end of a roll of pastry and made Phil take the other. They covered the pie trays as though with a sheet. Then Wix started cutting round each with a knife.

'Can I do that?'

Wix got another knife. 'You start that end. A nice neat cut, no hurry.' Phil worked happily.

70

'Dad,' Noel said. He had been looking after the fire. He came to the table and started gathering up the pastry off-cuts. 'We found a benzine can today. Motor spirit. With holes chopped in. Phil and me.'

Wix stopped cutting. 'Where?'

'Sunk in the creek. Buck's Hole.'

'Just down from Marwick's place,' Phil said.

'We reckon Mr. Marwick must be the fire-raiser.'

'That's jumping a bit far,' Wix said. 'Big can?'

'Five gallon. Marwick's is the closest house.'

Wix set to with his knife again. He finished the pies and started crimping them. He gave Phil a fork. 'Here, Phil, bung a hole in top. Who have you told?' he asked Noel.

'No one yet.' He wondered if he should tell his father about Kitty and Marwick, but decided not to. He felt it would take away from the importance of the can.

His father finished the pies and waited till Phil had made the holes. He slid them into the oven and closed the door.

'It's something I think McCaa should know. Tomorrow's Saturday, so I'll take you round. All right with you, young fellow?' he asked Phil.

'Yes,' Phil said. 'What are we going to do with this spare dough? Can we make some tarts?' He was intoxicated with the nearness of food.

Wix laughed. 'I'll tell you what. We'll knock up a couple of pasties. That can be your pay.'

◆

Kitty had not enjoyed her meal with the Chalmers family. Every time she saw Nancy Dormer, the big sister of one of her friends at school, dressed up as a maid, she felt herself blush. It seemed wrong, and more wrong still when Nancy called her 'Miss'. And the food was not very good, not as good as her mother made, and there was not enough — but no one offered second helpings.

'Don't breathe so loudly, Nancy,' Mrs. Chalmers said. 'We don't really need to know you're there.' Kitty blushed harder. She heard her own breathing after that.

Things got better in the parlor after dinner, when she and Irene sat far away at the other end of the room and took turns with Irene's kaleidoscope while Mr. Chalmers read the newspaper and Mrs. Chalmers did embroidery.

'Ha!' said Chalmers. 'That's good!'

'What?'

'Sir John French says the war will be won in three months.'

'It should go on longer, to teach the Germans a lesson,' Mrs. Chalmers said.

Irene and Kitty took no notice of that conversation. They had laid the kaleidoscope down and crept behind a sofa, and there they talked about Edgar Marwick. It seemed to them their proof was better than the boys', but the boys could show their can and Kitty had nothing to show. It would only be her word against Marwick's.

'What we need,' Irene said, 'is a way of telling on him without anyone knowing it's us.'

'Anonymous,' Kitty said. 'We could write "fire-raiser" on his gate.'

'No. I've got it. Wait here.' Irene went away and Kitty stayed sitting behind the sofa. In a moment Irene was back. She had writing paper and pencil and envelope. 'We'll write a letter to the police, but not put our names.'

She knelt on the floor and printed in square letters: 'Mr.

Marwick burnt down Dargie's Stables.' Kitty grabbed the pencil. 'We saw him.'

'What shall we sign it?'

Kitty grinned. Boldly she wrote: 'Britannia'.

'Now you.'

Irene wrote: 'Gallant Little Belgium'. They felt very clever and wanted to add more things, but in the end left it as it was. There was a bareness in it that made them shiver. They felt that Marwick must know and was lurking round the house.

'How are we going to get it to the police?'

'Post it. There's a box on the corner.'

Neither of them wanted to go out in the dark. They put the letter in the envelope and sealed it. Kitty wrote the address: 'Sergeant McCaa, Jessop Police Station', and printed 'Urgent' in the corner. 'It won't need a stamp.' She looked out the window at the dark. 'We could wait till morning.'

'It's better now. No one will see us.'

Kitty swallowed. The letter seemed to bulge as though something inside was trying to get out. 'Do you think he knows?'

'He didn't look at you.'

But for Irene, too, Marwick was close, with his green-eyed face and loping run and upraised arm. She thought of him as silent, quick, and mad.

Then suddenly her mother was by the sofa, and both girls gave a little scream.

'What are you girls up to?'

'Oh, Mrs. Chalmers,' Kitty said, 'you gave us such a fright!'

'What are you doing?'

Irene had taken the letter and turned it over so her mother would not see the address. 'It's homework. Letter writing,' she said.

'Let me see.'

'You gave us such a fright,' Kitty said. She had not known she could talk in such a la-di-da way. But it wasn't going to work. Mrs. Chalmers reached out her hand. 'Give it to me.'

They were saved by a shout, and by a thunderous knocking on the front door. Chalmers started up from his chair. 'What on earth! I'll go, Anne.' He went out quickly, paper in hand, and Mrs. Chalmers followed into the hall.

'Come on, quick,' Irene said. She led Kitty out another door and through the dining room into the kitchen. Nancy had gone home. They let themselves into the garden and ran across the lawn and through a side gate and reached the street a short way along from the house, hearing quick voices at the front door. Soft-footed, they ran to the letterbox on the corner. Irene pushed the letter in and they heard it whisper down on top of others. 'There. Done it.'

'Listen! That's the firebell,' Kitty said. The sound came distantly from the center of town. 'No, it's the engine.'

Chalmers ran out the gate and climbed with two men into a car. It came along towards the girls and screeched to a halt. Chalmers leaned out the door. 'What are you girls doing? Get back home.'

Mrs. Chalmers was calling from the gate. They ran to her. 'What's happened?'

'How dare you go out like that? You won't have friends again, Irene, if this is how you behave.'

'What's happened?'

'Your father's warehouse is on fire.'

CHAPTER SIX

At Chalmers' Warehouse

HE HAD SPENT a night and a day brooding on his wrongs. His fire at Dargie's seemed a feeble thing, far away in the past. He made no decision to go out again, but found himself preparing — rags and crowbar and benzine in a sack, old jacket ready on a hook in the barn, with the red balaclava in the pocket. He did not choose a building. He simply found it ready in his mind.

Before leaving, he went into the house to look at his mother. A sound of music came down the hall, a sound of voices wailing in love or grief. He stood under the hall chandelier, with its lusters sparkling like jewels, and listened a moment. The record ended. He heard her winding the gramophone, then it started again, the same record, tenor and soprano howling away. He curled his lip, and opened the door a few inches. The music swelled and he pushed the door open further and looked in. His mother sat in her chair with her stick on her knees. Her head was tilted, cheek on hand, and tears dripped from her chin on to her bodice. He had a moment of pity for her, pity and love, and pushed it away like the music. He closed the door and left her there, with silver tears rolling on her cheeks.

He picked up his gear from the barn and put on his jacket and slipped into the night. The town seemed hostile, like a fortress. He picked his way in by secret ways — across the railway bridge, down back alleys, over a silent park where children's swings creaked in the breeze, and seesaws and slides climbed to nowhere. He went through a building site, sliding on piles of sand, and climbed a bank into palm trees that sharpened their sword-leaves on each other. There, in the dark, he took out his balaclava and pulled it on. It was not for disguise; it was his sign. It seemed to light a fire in his head. Nothing would turn him back once it enclosed him.

The brick wall at Chalmers' warehouse stood six feet tall. He heaved his sack on top, hearing the benzine slop and the can boom faintly. He climbed and squatted, baboon-like, then dropped into the yard and pulled down his sack. The weight of it, the liquid weight, made him ache with anticipation, and the building, with its yellow bricks and beautiful dry wood, beckoned him. He ran to it. He saw his reflection dimly in a window, a flash of teeth, a ball of fire in place of his head. 'Ha!' he said, and stepped close to himself. He took his crowbar out of the sack.

'Now, Chalmers, you're going to get it! You'll see what I can do.'

◆

Noel and Phil came strolling down the street and stopped on a corner under a gas lamp. They were eating pasties, Phil more hungrily than Noel, who had already had his evening meal. Phil crunched the last pastry and licked his fingers.

'Your old man makes good stuff.'

Noel broke off a corner of his pastry. 'Have a bit.'

'Thanks.' Phil took it and gobbled. 'I reckon it'd be great being a baker.'

'Clippy reckons you should go to college.'

'Yeah, I know. It's all right for you jokers. I've got to go to work and earn some money.'

'He reckons you could be top of the class.'

'What for?' Phil belched to show his indifference, but Noel saw he was pleased.

'You could be something rich. A doctor, eh?'

'Fixing boils and sores. I'd rather be a baker.'

'How about a scientist? That's what I want to be.'

'Yeah, making stink bombs. That'd be okay.'

A muffled thud, a tinkling of glass, came from the looming bulk of Chalmers' warehouse. The boys jerked round, peering into the dark, then looked at each other.

'That was inside.'

'Burglars?'

'It could be the fire-raiser.'

They stood a moment, wondering what to do. The building was silent.

'We should get the police,' Noel said.

'What if it's just a cat?' Phil made up his mind. 'I'm going to have a look.' He ran silently on his bare feet down the alley at the side of the warehouse and waited for Noel at a place where dirt was heaped against the brick wall. 'Give us a lift.'

Noel made a step of his hands and heaved Phil up. 'See anything?'

'No.' Phil pulled himself on to the top of the wall. He sat with a leg dangling on each side. 'It's dark in there.' He hauled Noel by his shirt until he got a leg over. They sat together on the wall, waiting for something to happen.

'Must have been a cat,' Noel whispered.

'Maybe.' Phil dropped into the yard. Noel took off his shoes and socks and left them on the wall. He lowered himself beside Phil and they crouched in the shadows. Then they scuttled across to the warehouse wall. Noel caught a glint on the cobbles. 'Glass. Watch out.'

'Someone's jimmied the window,' Phil whispered. He looked at the cracked frame and broken pane. 'He must be in there.'

They crouched at the window, looking down the long cave of the building. High dusty windows let in light that barely reached the grain sacks and the bins. Alcoves, fissures black as pitch, opened on the sides. Nothing moved. Tiny rustlings and scuttlings came, mouse sounds, and the building creaked in the breeze, but that was all.

'There's no one here,' Noel whispered.

Then a match scraped. A sheet of flame flapped across the grain sacks. A man stood in it, arms raised, fiery-headed, red and black. He screeched like an owl. He was like the devil.

'The fire-raiser,' Noel yelled.

He swung on them. His eyes were like cat eyes in the night; they were tunnels deep into his head. He charged at them, outlined in a band of fire, then swung aside and burst the double doors open with his foot. The boys ran to the corner and saw him come tumbling into the yard. He had lost his flames and was ordinary — a man in boots and ragged jacket and red balaclava.

'Get him,' Phil yelled.

They ran at him and tried to grab his jacket but he batted Noel away with a blow of his arm, then plucked Phil off his back and threw him skidding across the cobbles. He ran to the wall and hauled himself up. Noel was lying dazed, but Phil came up on hands and knees, saw the man, ran across the yard and seized his trouser leg. The fire-raiser kicked him away and went over the top. His boots smacked on the pavement and beat off into the night. Phil stood up. He had cracked his head and took a moment to know where he was. Then he jumped for the top of the wall, but could not hold his grip and fell back. He turned to shout to Noel, and saw Chalmers' warehouse all lit up. Noel was there, by the double doors, uncoiling the hose from the wall, coupling it to the tap, trying to haul it into the building.

'Help me with this!'

Phil ran to him and they pulled the hose through the door. They shielded themselves and came close to the fire until it seemed to peel the skin from their faces.

'Turn it on!'

Phil ran back to the yard and turned on the tap. He looked inside and saw Noel standing against the flames, shooting a jet of water into them. It made no difference. 'Get the brigade,' Noel screamed.

Phil climbed the padlocked gates. He ran through the streets and came to the firebell and rang it madly. 'Fire!' he yelled. 'Fire! Chalmers' warehouse.'

Then he seemed to have no part in things. Men took over. He found himself standing by the bell, with the rope in his hand, and saw the engine shriek past, and he trotted back to the warehouse, and there was Noel standing in the yard, and the fat firehose snaking inside. Only a small glow came from in there. The gates were open, Chalmers was running about, Mr. Wix was patting Noel's head, and Clippy Hedges was saying, 'Every time I look at Mars there seems to be a fire.'

'Out of the way, boy. Get off home,' Sergeant McCaa said.

'No,' Noel said. 'He was here. He helped me.' Then Noel explained and the men all listened, and Hedges patted Phil on the back.

Chalmers said, 'I can't thank you boys enough.'

'We saw him. We tried to catch him. He kicked my face,' Phil said.

'It was him all right.' McCaa had a benzine can and a crowbar in his hands. 'Did you see who it was?'

'He was wearing a red thing on his head.'

'A balaclava,' Noel said. 'We couldn't see his face.'

'Not very well.'

McCaa looked at him. He could tell Phil wanted to say more. Noel blurted it out. 'We think it was Mr. Marwick.'

'Marwick?'

'You could tell by his eyes,' Phil said.

'I hope you boys know what you're saying.'

'We found a motor spirits can by his place. In Buck's Hole.'

'And so you put two and two together.' McCaa looked at Mr. Wix. 'I don't like this.'

'They wouldn't say it lightly,' Wix said.

McCaa rounded on the boys. 'You didn't see his face? Just his eyes?'

'Yes,' Noel said.

'Did you hear his voice?'

'No.'

'You?' to Phil.

'No.'

McCaa turned to Wix and Chalmers. 'This is no good.'

'Marwick was in my office yesterday,' Chalmers said. 'I won't say he threatened me, but we had some difference of opinion. He was very angry when he left.'

McCaa thought that over. He banged the can on his leg. 'All right. I'll talk to him. You boys come. I'd better have you too, Mr. Wix.'

'I'll come, Sergeant,' Hedges said.

'Why?'

Hedges tapped Phil's head. 'In loco parentis for this boy.'

So they drove out to Marwick's farm in the sergeant's car. The night was dark except for a blade of moon low in the sky. They boomed over the wooden bridge down-river from Buck's Hole and came to the big old silent house. Light streamed over the veranda from the living room. The sergeant parked his car and creaked on the handbrake. Soon they were inside, facing Edgar Marwick and Mrs. Marwick. They stood just inside the door in a group: McCaa, Wix, Hedges, Noel and Phil. The door was ajar and the long hall stretched on either side, and they were outsiders who had penetrated this far by mistake and stood confused and ready to run: so it seemed to the boys. Edgar Marwick, who had let them in, had gone to a place by his mother's winged chair and stood there butler-like, neat and tidy, curious, cool. Mrs. Marwick sat like a queen, an ancient, dry-boned, beak-nosed queen, and held her stick across her knees as though she might suddenly point and order someone's death. Green beads glittered on her breast. Her black shoes had silver buckles. The boys swallowed and wet their lips. But McCaa was unafraid. He spoke as though this were an ordinary visit.

'Good evening, Ma'am. I'm sorry to disturb you at this hour.'

Mrs. Marwick took no notice. 'Close the door. I'm in a draft.'

Hedges nudged Phil, who closed it quickly.

'This is quite an invasion. You're the sergeant at the police station, is that right?'

'McCaa,' said McCaa. 'It's Mr. Marwick I have to talk with. I can do it in another room if you like.'

'No, no, I'm curious. And all these people with you?'

'I'll come to that.' He looked at Marwick. 'I'd like to know where you've been tonight.'

Marwick raised his chin. He was taller than the sergeant and looked down with an expression of mild indignation. 'You've no right to ask me that.'

'Explain it to me, sergeant. It is rather odd,' Mrs. Marwick said.

'Yes, Ma'am. Someone tried to burn down Chalmers' warehouse. These boys saw him.' He turned back to Marwick. 'They think it was you, Mr. Marwick.'

'That's damned nonsense!' Marwick said. 'You come here bothering me because of a couple of town boys!' His heavy face had taken on a fierce look and his green eyes glowed.

McCaa kept his voice uninflected. 'Do you own a red balaclava, Mr. Marwick?'

Only Hedges was watching Mrs. Marwick. He saw a widening of her eyes. The pupils seemed to expand, then shrink; the irises closed like sea anemones. That was all. She was still. She seemed bored.

'Balaclava?' Marwick said.

'A woollen garment. Covers the head.'

'I know what a balaclava is.' Bad-temperedly.

McCaa was dogged. 'Do you own a coat, sir? Black over-coat, full length. Elbows out. No buttons.'

'No, I don't.'

'It's hardly the sort of thing my son would wear,' Mrs. Marwick said. 'Or a balaclava. You should be looking for some tramp or swagger. I don't care for this, sergeant.'

'I'm sorry, Ma'am.' McCaa was not going to be put off. He unwrapped the cloth in his hands and showed the crow-bar and can. 'Have you seen these before?' he asked Mar-wick.

'No. Should I?'

'What are they, Sergeant?'

'A crowbar, Ma'am. And a motor spirits can. They were left at the scene of the fire.'

'And you think they belong to my son? Are they yours, Edgar?'

'Of course they're not. I don't use motor spirits. Got no use for it. And I've got three or four crowbars in the shed.'

'Well, Sergeant, is that enough?'

'One more thing.' To Edgar he said, 'A can was found in the river by your farm.'

It was Mrs. Marwick who replied. Sharply, pushing out her face, she said, 'My farm. It belongs to me. And since the pools were opened, all sorts of riff-raff get in. Look some-where else.' She lifted her stick and prodded at Noel and Phil. 'Look at these boys. I wouldn't be surprised if they lit the fire and are wriggling out.'

They felt as if a bolt of lightning had come out of the stick. McCaa looked at them thoughtfully.

'That's not true,' Noel cried.

'We saw a man. Even if it wasn't Mr. Marwick,' Phil said.

'Oh, they're not sure now,' Mrs. Marwick said.

Nobody was taking any notice of Thomas Hedges. He had drifted away from the group at the door, and suddenly he stepped close to Edgar Marwick. 'Can I see your hands, Mr. Marwick?'

'What?' Marwick half raised his hands, as though Hedges was about to attack him, and Hedges seized his wrist and looked at it. Marwick jerked away. A sound of anger started in his throat, but McCaa stepped forward.

'What do you think you're doing, Hedges? Come here. In fact, get out. You've no authority.'

'Look at the backs of his hands. The hairs are singed. He's been lighting fires.'

'I was burning rubbish. Out in the yard. See for yourself,' Marwick said. And Mrs. Marwick added in her thrilling voice, making it ring, 'The ashes are still hot if you want to see. Now this has gone far enough. My son has been home all night, in this room with me, working on accounts. So please go away. Out of my house.'

McCaa had seen Edgar Marwick's wrists. He stood undecided.

'You're not going to doubt my word, Sergeant?'

'No Ma'am, of course not,' McCaa said.

'Then I'll say it again, out of my house. And if you want my advice you'll question these boys. Edgar, show them out.' She raised her stick and pointed at the hall.

◆

Edgar Marwick waited until the sound of the car died away, then he turned and walked back to the parlor and opened the door. He did not face her, but knew she was watching him. He closed the door, keeping his back to her, waiting for the silence to break. After a time he looked at her over his shoulder.

She had a faint smile on her face. Evenly she said, 'Fires, Edgar? I thought you'd finished with all that.'

He turned and faced her, with his back to the door. He looked at her from under his brows, like a child, afraid, in disgrace, but still defiant.

'Come here, Edgar. Sit down.' She tapped the sofa with her stick.

He disobeyed. Things revolved about her. They fell into the places she chose for them. He would not do it. He moved about the room.

'I hate dark places.'

'Sit down. Be still.'

'You locked me in. You wouldn't let me come out in the light.'

Mrs. Marwick shook her head impatiently. 'I punished you, Edgar, because of Lucy. You were supposed to watch, and you didn't watch.'

He crept at her, almost kneeling. 'You locked me in the cupboard. In the dark. I heard the key.'

'You had to be punished.'

'It was like locking up my eyes. It was being buried.'

Flatly, angrily, she said, 'You should have watched her.'

He did not hear. 'But I beat you. I lit fires. In here. In my head.'

'I know you burned the outhouse down. Your father whipped you for that.'

'More.' He banged his head with his fists. 'I burned the churches. I burned the banks. I burned the whole town.'

He thrust his face at her. 'And now I'm grown up I really do it.'

'You're not grown up. Forty-five and still a boy.' She put her stick on his shoulder and held him still. It made him blink. 'No more fires. It's got to stop.'

He fell into sulkiness and watched her again from under his brows.

'Where's the balaclava?'

He shook his head.

'Give it to me.'

'No. It's mine.'

'Edgar — '

'I put it away.'

She watched him, the hulking man who had never grown into a man. Then she tapped him with the ferrule of her stick and pushed him away. 'No more fires. Or I'll let them put you in prison. You won't like that. It's dark in there.'

CHAPTER SEVEN

The Ram

MRS. CHALMERS MADE a ceremony of morning tea, but her husband had no time for it today. He sipped and scalded his lips, and swore under his breath, and blew in his cup.

'Francis!'

'I'm sorry, my dear, but I've got to get down and see if they're cleaning up.'

'That's no excuse for blowing on your tea.'

Kitty, on the sofa, followed this with interest. Irene gave a little smirking grin. She was not embarrassed by her parents but treated their contests as a sporting event, which she liked her father to win. She wished he would be as tough about her — about the piano for instance — as he sometimes was about his business.

'Girls, you may take a biscuit,' Mrs. Chalmers said.

They took one, and Kitty almost felt she should curtsy. 'Thank you, Mrs. Chalmers. And thank you for having me.'

Mrs. Chalmers inclined her head. 'Your brother behaved very well last night. It's a pity though he made such an accusation. How anyone could think the Marwicks were involved . . .'

Kitty and Irene sent a look at each other. They remembered their letter.

'He's a funny fellow, Marwick, all the same,' Chalmers said.

'They're a very good family. What happened to those boys?'

'McCaa took them to the station. Got a statement. Not that there's any good in it. It's understandable they got carried away. Still, they saved my warehouse.' He sipped his tea. 'Too hot. Come along, Kitty. I'll drop you on my way.'

'Can I come too? And go to Kitty's?' Irene said.

'May I, not can I,' Mrs. Chalmers said. 'No, I think not.'

'We want to practice our pageant speeches,' Kitty said. The idea came to her out of the air. 'Irene helps with my pronunciation.'

That pleased Mrs. Chalmers. She gave a smile. 'Very well. Just a short time. See that you behave, Irene.'

'Yes, Mother,' Irene said meekly. 'We'll get Kitty's bag.' The girls went out.

'I'm not sure I like it,' Mrs. Chalmers said. 'She is rather common.'

'Nonsense, Anne,' Chalmers said. 'It does Irene good. She's got some color in her cheeks.'

◆

Phil had been at the wharves, watching the pilot bring in a freighter. She was a tub with rust patches on her sides, and she made him think of a poem Clippy had read: 'Dirty British coaster with a salt-caked smoke stack, Butting through the Channel in the mad March days. . . .' He didn't know what mad March days were, but he could see *this* freighter butting at waves, burying her snout and heaving up, with water streaming from her, and he composed a future for himself in which he was cabin boy, then mate, then master, swinging on the wheel and fighting typhoons.

Later, he had walked to the rivermouth and watched the tide running over the mudflats. He followed the river into the town. Men were cleaning up in Chalmers' warehouse. He watched them for a while, and saw Chalmers arrive in his flash car and start giving orders, and his own part in the fire seemed to sink into the past and become very small. He went on and hung around outside the Wix house. Noel saw him from a window and came out. They walked down to the footbridge and leaned on the rail, watching for trout and talking about the fire.

'My dad believes us. So does Clippy,' Noel said.

'Makes no difference,' Phil said. 'That sergeant's a bugger. He reckons we did it.' He was bitter. 'I'd love to get that old tart, Mrs. Marwick.'

'We need evidence,' Noel said.

'Yeah. We should get Sherlock Holmes.'

Noel was offended. 'We could go out to the farm. Sneak in the back.'

'For what? Here's Charmy-Barmy. Quit following us,' Phil yelled. Irene and Kitty were advancing along the bridge.

'We can walk here. It's not your bridge,' Irene said. She did not want to be unfriendly to Phil. 'My father wants to give you a shilling.'

'Tell him to keep it.'

'What about me?' Noel said.

'You'll get half a crown,' Phil said sourly.

'Did you tell them about the benzine can?' Kitty said.

'Yeah. No good.'

'Maybe they'll believe when they get our letter,' Irene said.

'What letter?'

'We wrote to the police.'

'We said it was Mr. Marwick.'

'Did you sign it?' Phil asked.

Kitty grinned. 'Britannia.'

'Belgium,' Irene said.

Phil was impressed, but said, 'That's dumb. They'll work that out. Anyhow, we're going to get some evidence.'

'Where?'

'Marwick's farm. You coming?' he asked Noel. He was fretting to try something, do something real.

'Sure,' Noel said. He followed Phil along the bridge.

'We're coming too,' Kitty said. She and Irene ran to catch up.

'No you're not.'

'You can't stop us,' Irene said.

'It's not your business.'

'He knocked me over. Twice,' Kitty said.

'They'll be all right,' Noel said. 'They can keep watch.'

'They'll get caught, that's what'll happen,' Phil said. It seemed to him that, compared to Noel and the girls, he was grown up.

They took the dirt road to Marwick's farm and crossed the one-way bridge and turned up the river towards Buck's Hole. The front paddocks were empty, but the ones sloping into the hills beyond the farmhouse were dotted with sheep. The house did not have its fairy castle appearance today; it seemed big and ugly and threatening. The windows in the bows were like bulbous eyes watching them. They passed the hole and followed the river up towards the rapids, and the yard of Marwick's farm opened up.

'There he is.'

Edgar Marwick, wearing a red shirt, moved from a shed to some contraption set up in the yard, and stood there working his leg up and down. They could not tell what he was doing, but anything Marwick did seemed sinister.

'We've got to get him out of there,' Phil said.

'How?'

They moved up-river. A regular, flat thumping sounded above the noise of the rapids.

'What's that?' Irene said.

'His ram.'

Irene stopped.

'Hydraulic ram,' Noel said. 'It won't bite you.'

They passed the rapids and came to the machine bolted to a platform. The intake pipe snaked from the fast-flowing water and the feed-pipe to the house ran off in a straight line over a paddock. Clap, clap, clap, went a valve, like a heart beating. An air chamber, swollen like a fat man, sat in the center.

'What makes it go?' Irene said.

'Water momentum,' Noel said. 'It closes this valve and the water gets forced up into the chamber and along the pipe. Then the valve falls open and it all happens again.' He enjoyed explaining things, liked feeling clever. 'Simple,' he said.

Phil had been in the scrub, watching Edgar Marwick. He came back and looked at the ram. 'We'll jam it,' he said.

'What for?'

Phil jerked his thumb at Irene and Kitty. 'They'll jam it. When he comes to fix it we do a search.'

'I'm coming too,' Kitty said.

'If you like.' Phil did not mind Kitty, it was Irene he didn't like. 'Do you reckon you can do it, Charmy-Barmy?'

'Of course,' Irene said. She was disappointed with Kitty and felt betrayed.

'You have to stop this valve.'

'How?'

'Bit of wood. Bit of wire.'

Irene, wanting to be more important than Kitty, took a hairpin from her hair. 'Will this do?'

'Yeah. Good. You stick it in here, in the hinge. Stop this thing from moving. Not till you see us by the barn. When you see him coming, clear right out.' He grinned. 'If he catches you, he'll eat you for his breakfast.'

Irene curled her lip. 'I'm not scared.' She was terrified. Kitty grinned at her, but she looked away. She sat down by the water with her back to the ram, and only when the three had sneaked away, jumped up and ran a few steps after them. She wanted to see them for as long as she could. Phil looked back. 'Don't forget to take the hairpin out.'

They kept below the riverbank, circling the farm. A tongue of bush ran into a paddock and they followed it and came within twenty yards of the barn. 'What's he doing?'

'Sharpening tools.'

Edgar Marwick had a grinding wheel set up on a trestle and cutting tools spread out on the ground. He was sharppening a sickle. The wheel grated like a dentist's drill as he worked the treadle. A stream of sparks played on his hands.

'Come on.'

They crept in the bush and the edge of the barn moved round and hid him from sight. They ran for the barn, bent at the waist — and Irene, in the scrub by the river, saw them cross the band of grass like three galloping dwarfs. She saw them at the corner of the barn, stacked almost on top of each other, peering round at Edgar Marwick. Now she had to jam the valve.

She went back through the scrub to the ram and saw it sitting there, ugly and fat, and felt it would snap at her, defend itself. She still had the hairpin in her fingers and she sneaked up on it as though it were someone she had to surprise and prick with the points. Clap, clap, thump, thump, it went. She saw the valve working like a tongue, greedily, and she almost closed her eyes as she stabbed at it. The pin went in. She wondered why the ram didn't squeal. But it was worse than that. It was suddenly dead. In the silencing of its tongue, she heard the river rushing. Water gushed like blood through the open valve. She jerked her hand away and wiped it on her dress.

In the yard Edgar Marwick finished one side of the sickle. He turned it round. Water had stopped spurting into the tank at the side of the house but the absence of the noise did not strike him. He turned the wheel and ran the sickle blade across it. The children watched from behind the barn. He was side on to them and the comet-tail of sparks ran up his arm into the crook of his elbow.

'She must have done it by now,' Noel whispered.

'She's messed it up. Probably wet her pants,' Phil said.

'She'll do it,' Kitty said. 'Look! He's stopped. He knows something's wrong.'

Edgar Marwick laid down the sickle. He held his head up, as though sniffing the wind. He swung round in a half circle, not looking for anything, but trying to find what troubled him. Then he had it; silence in the tank. He strode to it, leaped up on the stand, hauled himself upright. He jerked the hose out of its hole, and swore, and rammed it back. He leaned out like a shunter on an engine, looking at the river, his face as red as his shirt, then he jumped down and strode away with yard-long strides. He vaulted a fence, kicked a thistle, hacked it with his heel, strode on, making for the river.

They watched him climb another fence.

'Now,' Phil said. They ran round to the double doors of the barn. 'Kitty, you keep watch.'

'What are we looking for?' Noel said.

'Benzine. Rags. Anything. That red balaclava.'

'I'm going to look in the shed,' Kitty said.

'OK. But watch out for him.'

The boys went in and Kitty slipped across to the door of a shed close to the house. Edgar Marwick kept his tools inside. She had a last look at him and saw him approaching the scrub by the river, and thought she glimpsed the blue of Irene's dress moving in the teatree. She hoped Irene was getting away, but there really wasn't time to worry about her. She went into the shed and started rummaging in corners.

In the teatree Irene watched Edgar Marwick approach. She remembered him from the time in her father's office and on the steps when he had knocked Kitty flying. Then he had seemed wild and dangerous, but now, as he grew taller crossing the paddock, as his boots ate up the land, he was like someone from a nightmare. He was magical, terrifying; she felt he could strip the bushes away with his eyes and uncover her, and reach out with an arm and pick her up. She almost felt his hand squeezing her. She imagined she could hear his boots and feel the ground trembling. Irene was used to managing adults, but knew that here was one she would never control. It was like being shown that beyond grownups was another group of beings, magical and powerful and not to be approached. She began to creep backwards, and was surprised to find her legs carrying her. When she could see him no longer she turned and ran to the riverbank. She approached the pot-bellied ram with a sidling step, scared of it too, and seized the pin and gave it a jerk.

It would not come out.

It was as if a hand in there was pulling against her. She gave another jerk, but it stayed fixed, and she gave a whimper of fright and looked through the scrub. Edgar Marwick's red shirt bobbed up and down as he climbed the last fence.

Irene knew she had no more time. She left the hairpin and scuttled sideways like a crab, and tipped herself down a bank almost into the water. A willow tree stood there, with half its roots reaching out like fingers, and she wriggled under them and found she could stand in a little chamber and see through a crack in the turf all the way back at ground level to the ram. Edgar Marwick came through the teatree. She saw him from his waist down, and saw him pause two steps from the ram — he had seen the pin — and come on with a single stride, and saw his hand reach down and give a jerk and the pin came free. She wondered why the ram did not start up, but it stayed silent. She heard Marwick grunt, and swear; a word she hadn't heard before, but she knew it was filthy. From the way his feet moved, she knew he was hunting with his eyes. He was only ten steps from her and she saw him take those steps, and stand above her, she almost felt his hand leaning on the tree. His boots were only six inches from her nose. She stayed as still as a lizard, but her heart was banging; as loud as the ram it banged, and she couldn't understand why Edgar Marwick didn't hear. He kicked the ground and fine gravel came through the crack and stung her lips. He swore again, and turned and went off in his loping half-run, and she saw the hairpin shining in his fingers as he disappeared in the scrub.

Irene stayed where she was. She did not move for a long time. She could not be sure he would not come back. At last she crept out, and she crawled through rabbit trails in the scrub, and lay on her belly, lower than the grass-tops, watching the barn. She saw Kitty come running out of a shed by the house.

◆

Noel and Phil had searched the barn, gone right round the walls, shifted everything that would shift, looked behind everything. Now they sat on the huge hay pile that occupied it — they had climbed it like a mountain — wondering what to do next.

'We better get out. He could come back.'

'Quiet a minute.' Phil listened. 'We don't have to go till the water starts in the tank.'

Noel wondered why he hadn't thought of that. He didn't like the way Phil was having all the ideas.

'There's nothing here. We should look in the house.'

'Not with the old tart in there. He wouldn't keep benzine inside, anyway.'

Noel looked round again. The air was thick with dust and soon his hay fever would start. Then he saw a little door in the wall, half buried in hay. 'Did you look in there?'

'Didn't see it,' Phil said.

They slid down the pile and cleared hay in armfuls from the door. It stood chest high and was only two feet wide, fastened with a bolt. Phil worked it loose and opened the door. A grain sack covered something like a blanket. Phil pulled it aside. Two large cans of benzine stood on the floor, with smaller ones clustered round. A pile of cotton waste and rags lay at the back.

The boys let out a sigh. 'That's it. We've got him.'

'There's a funnel. He fills one of the small cans when he goes out for a fire.'

'Yeah,' Phil breathed. 'Now that sergeant's going to say he's sorry.'

'What do we do? Take it with us?'

'Leave it here. We bring him out.'

'He won't come. He won't believe us.'

'Get Kitty. She can see.'

Noel stood up and started round the hay. Then he stopped. Footfalls sounded on the hard-packed earth of the yard. Edgar Marwick appeared in the door. He stood, red and ogrish, arms akimbo, legs wide. He seemed to blot out all the light from outside. A noise began in his throat and swelled into a shout of rage that echoed in the barn.

97

'Marwick!' Noel yelled. He ran back to Phil. 'Split up.' He kept going back along the wall. Phil scrambled up the stack and squatted on top. He saw Edgar Marwick still in the door, and saw him start in, and pluck a hayfork from the wall as he went by. He got ready to run down to the door, but Marwick changed direction and started up, using the fork to anchor himself on the slope.

'Look out!' Noel yelled.

It brought Marwick round with a suddenness that made Noel trip as he turned to run, but he jumped up and went along the chasm between wall and hay, past a padlocked door in the back of the barn. Instead of sloping upwards, the hay made a cliff that could not be climbed, and at the far wall it was packed in tight, leaving no gap for him to go through. He heard Marwick panting. In a moment he would come round the corner and Noel would be trapped at the end of an alley. He dived at the hay and burrowed in. Deep in he went, pulling hay after him, hiding himself. Then he stopped. His nose was running from the dust, but he knew he mustn't sneeze or make a sound. He heard Edgar Marwick stepping softly, and then a hissing sound that froze his blood — the sound of fork prongs sliding in hay. Everything was changed. Adults were brutal, and the game had turned to death. A step had been taken that changed the nature of things. Tears burst from his eyes. He opened his mouth in a soundless howl. Then he heard a distant yell, and heard something crack against the wall, and Marwick bellow.

Phil had seen the danger; Marwick stepping like a wading bird, head moving, this way and that, the fork stabbing beak-like into the hay. From a little half-loft in the roof he grabbed a handful of rusty six-inch nails, an old whetstone, a broken door-hinge, and scrambled for a better view, then started pelting Marwick; first the hinge, then the whetstone, last the nails, one by one, like daggers. A nail struck, chipping skin from Marwick's forearm. The man gave a cry, of disbelief as much as pain. He ran back to the corner and along the side of the barn, and started up the easier slope at Phil. At that moment a piercing call came from outside the barn. 'Edgar!'

He stopped. He listened.

'Edgar! What's happening in there?'

Marwick glared at Phil. He held up the fork and prodded it in his direction. 'You wait there. I've got you.' He turned and walked to the door.

◆

When Kitty heard the first bellow from the barn she ran out of the shed and went a few steps in that direction, then changed her mind and jumped up on the veranda of the house. She ran along it, hoping to see into the barn from there, but all she could see was a slope of hay. A voice, her brother's, yelled, 'Look out!' Then there was silence. She could not imagine what was happening. Marwick must be back, but why the silence? She looked towards the river and saw nothing, no Irene there. Then cracks and bangs started in the barn, hard things hitting a wall, and Marwick's voice gave another yell. She made up her mind to go and see, but as she began to move, the door on her left started to open. She had time to run a few steps and hide behind a wicker rockingchair before Mrs. Marwick came on to the veranda. The old lady called her son, called twice, shrill as a parrot.

He appeared in the barn door. Kitty, kneeling, saw him from under the chair.

'Those two town boys. I've got 'em cornered.'

'What are they doing in there?'

'I don't know. Pinching stuff.'

'Be careful, Edgar. Don't hurt them too much.'

'I'll hurt 'em.' He went back into the barn. Mrs. Marwick looked as if she would climb down from the veranda, but changed her mind and stood holding a post. Kitty backed away from her into a glassed-in part of the veranda, but found it blocked by a wall at the other end. It shocked her. She had expected to sneak down there and get away.

'Edgar! Edgar!' Mrs. Marwick shrieked.

Kitty looked through the glass to see what alarmed her. A Jersey bull stood in a pen at the back of the barn. She saw its wicked eyes and the rope of slobber from its chin. Then Noel was there, scrambling over the rail, with Phil behind him. They dropped into the yard and ran for the paddocks.

'Edgar, they came through the bull-pen. They got out through the loose board in the back,' Mrs. Marwick cried. She came to the corner to watch them better. She had only to turn her head to see Kitty. 'Chase them, Edgar. Run!' Kitty heard boots thud by the veranda. She heard the panting of a heavy man and the squeak of wires as he climbed a fence. Noel and Phil had a good start. She was sure they would get away. It was herself she was worried about. Perhaps she could run by the old lady — but her arms looked so wiry and strong. She would shriek for her son. And any second now, watching the chase, she would turn into the glassed-in part of the veranda.

Kitty took her only way of escape. Quietly, bent almost double, she opened a door and slipped into the house.

CHAPTER EIGHT

Kitty Plays the Piano

SHE HEARD A faint click as the door closed, and looked around to see where she was. It took a moment for her eyes to get used to the gloom, then she saw that she was in a hallway. Chandeliers of brass and glass hung from a ceiling so high she had a sudden fearful sense this house was made for giants. Big heavy chests and cupboards lined the walls. Pictures in carved frames hung from a rail — cattle with lowered heads, grey lakes, mountains that seemed horned. The trees and flowers had all their color faded out. A strip of floral carpet, dark red, dark blue, ran down the hall, and Kitty followed it, sliding her feet to make no sound. She tried a door handle, but it was locked and her hand came away coated with dust.

Suddenly the door she had come through opened. Light flooded the hall. Mrs. Marwick stood there, half in, half out, looking away through the veranda glass at Edgar Marwick chasing Noel and Phil. Kitty had no time. She was beside a second door and she took the handle, turned it, found the door unlocked. She pushed softly. It opened with no sound. She slipped in and closed the door behind her.

Now she was in a dark room. She stood with her back to the door, waiting for her eyes to adjust. There were shapes all about, like boulders, like cattle, but in a moment she saw sofas, chairs, sideboards, a black piano. The shimmering in the gloom was a brass fire-guard. She smelled dust and mold, and also caught a whiff of rot, perhaps a mouse or rat dead in a wall. Across the room was something she took for a huge door but when she saw it better it turned into red and gold drapes running almost from ceiling to floor. A door stood beyond the fireplace, on another wall. Kitty threaded her way to it, through the crowded furniture. It was locked, with no key in the keyhole. She turned to the drapes, pulled them open two or three inches. Dust rained down, silver in the sudden light. Kitty tried the window but the catch was rusted solid and would not move. The panes were frosted with dust and when she rubbed a circle, showed only dirt on the other side. She gave a little breath of fear. The only way out was through the door she had come in by.

Kitty stood in the corner and listened. She thought she heard steps padding in the hall, but was not sure. And the soft creaking — was that feet or noises of the house?

After a while she moved out of the corner. She saw better and her fear began to slip away as she looked at the room. Gloomy pictures, cousins of the ones in the hall, hung from a rail. Pockets of dust lay in their carved frames. Half a wall was taken up with books in a glass case, but she could not read their names and they did not look as if they were meant to be read. Their rounded backs seemed glued to each other. She drew a tiny flower in the dust on the glass. Then she looked at the framed photographs on the mantelpiece. And blinked. Went close. She was not wrong. Every photo was of the same girl. She was two or three here, eight or nine there, in clothes with lots of ribbons and frills, and smiling in one, serious in another — but the same girl. And there she was on the piano, too, in a bonnet like the one Miss Muffet wore in nursery-rhyme books. Kitty picked her up and looked at her. A pretty face, with a fat happy mouth. She looked as if she'd had lots of cake to eat. She didn't look the sort of girl who'd want to sit still for photographs.

Kitty put it down. She looked at the yellowed music on the piano and smiled as she saw scales she could do — easy scales. This girl could not have been very good. She touched a key and brought away her finger smudged with dust. Then she pushed the key down softly, B flat, wanting to make the softest velvet sound; but the key was dead. She kept her finger on it and felt a sponginess. It puzzled her. She threw a quick look at the door; released the key and pressed again, a little harder. No sound, and the sponginess still there. She felt as though someone had stuffed a cloth into her mouth.

Kitty shifted the photo of the girl to the back of the piano and lifted the lid. It came up easily, without a sound, and she held it with one hand and stood on tiptoes, trying to see the hammers and wires, but this was the tallest piano she had ever seen and she could not manage. With her free hand she edged the piano stool along the floor and climbed on it, standing with bent knees to keep it from revolving. Now she could see the innards. There was something red in there, like a liver or heart. She reached in, scared of spiders, and pulled it out. She let it fall open in her hand. A red balaclava. Her breath came sharply. It was like a cut-off head. It was the head of the man who had knocked her down.

The swivel stool made movements under her feet and she

felt slightly dizzy. She knelt, still holding the lid. She put the balaclava on the keys and unbuttoned her blouse. Carefully she put in the balaclava, though it made her feel dirty, made her itch. She buttoned up and pressed down the lump under the cloth, then she lowered the lid and shifted the photo of the girl in the bonnet back to its place. She put one of her feet on the floor. The seat of the stool made a quarter turn. It gave a wild shriek of pain.

Kitty almost fainted. She stood with mouth open, eyes shut, and heard a drumming silence in her ears. Then she held the seat with two hands and took her other knee off. She faced the door. It was no surprise to her when the handle started to turn.

The door opened slowly. Mrs. Marwick stood there, in black and purple dress and buckled shoes, with green beads cascading, with bony hands pressed to her abdomen. Then she stepped in and closed the door and the room turned darker. Only a little light came from the crack Kitty had left in the curtains. Mrs. Marwick's face seemed luminous. A faint humming came from her mouth, as though she were making changes in her head, lifting a kind of music up in pitch. To Kitty she seemed to go out of focus, and come back sharp and black, longer in her bones. She felt like screaming.

'Lucy, is that you?' Mrs. Marwick said.

Kitty stepped backwards along the mat. The old lady followed.

'Where have you been? I've been looking.'

She held out her hands, then dropped them to her sides. She smiled, showing teeth as yellow as the piano keys. 'Play for me, child. Do your scales.'

Kitty stood still. It was not just darkness confusing Mrs. Marwick. The old lady had gone back through years and years of time. Lucy was the girl in the photographs, and *she* was Lucy. The mistake was one of knowing, not of seeing, Kitty thought. She felt to put it right would be to place herself in worse danger. She looked at the piano. Those were easy scales.

Quickly she sat down. She began; exercises running up and down. If Irene thought the Wix piano was out of tune, she should try this one. It sounded, Kitty thought, like a wire fence. It was like the broken mandolin in the back of the wardrobe at home. But she played on, up and down the scales, and did not dare look at the old lady behind her. She heard springs twang as Mrs. Marwick sat on a sofa. When she was done she sat looking at her hands.

'Yes,' Mrs. Marwick said. That was all. The silence grew longer and longer. Kitty risked a look over her shoulder. Mrs. Marwick was sitting straight. Her eyes were blinking, puzzled, as though she began to see part of the truth. But she pushed it away, pushed it in a corner, and gave a smiling frown at Kitty. 'Keep on. You'll never get better if you don't try.'

Kitty played the scales again. Mrs. Marwick said, 'That was not very good. You must practice harder.'

'Yes,' Kitty whispered.

'Come and sit by me.' But again she had that puzzled look. She was on the point of coming back through the years — came a little way, then slipped into the time of Lucy again.

'Sit by your mother.'

Kitty threw a look at the door. If she could get there, she

could get outside. She had to be gone before Mrs. Marwick realized she was someone else. But boots tramped on the veranda before she could move. A door slammed at the other end of the house. Mrs. Marwick smiled.

'He's a noisy boy. Sit. Here.' She patted the sofa at her side, sending up a puff of dust. Kitty was more frightened of Edgar than of his mother. She sat down.

'Tell me about school, Lucy. What lessons did you have today?'

Kitty did not know what to say. 'Sums,' she whispered, hoping it was the proper word.

'Sums? Are you good at them? Are you working hard?'

'Yes.'

'I was good at sums. On the ship coming out we had our lessons in the salon. Mr. Gibbons took us. The minister. But oh, we were so seasick all the time. And sick with fever. Estelle Weaver died. And Tommy Gamble died. Poor wee things. They were buried at sea, wrapped in tarpaulins, side by side.' She had taken Kitty's hand and was stroking it. Her breath was on Kitty's face and had the same musty smell as the room. 'It was calm weather. And the sun was beating down. And the sails were lying on the masts and just going flap, flap, now and then, and my mother was crying. Estelle's mother tried to jump into the sea and men had to hold her. Grief is terrible, Lucy. A terrible thing.' Kitty said nothing. She looked at the old lady's hand stroking hers. She knew it would find her out, discover the truth, and bring Mrs. Marwick out of that time into now. And the fingers stopped their stroking. They felt. They squeezed. Snatched away. Mrs. Marwick gave a dreadful cry. She fastened her gaze on Kitty's face.

'You are not Lucy!'

'No,' Kitty whispered.

'Who are you?'

'Kitty Wix.'

'Where's Lucy?' It was a wail, a cry of grief.

'I don't know,' Kitty said.

Mrs. Marwick turned her face away. She wiped her hand across her cheeks. Kitty could not tell if she was crying, but when the old woman looked back, her eyes were dry. She said in an ordinary voice, 'Lucy was younger. How old are you?'

'Eleven.'

'Lucy was eight. She drowned in the river. Did you know?'

Kitty could not speak. She shook her head.

'It was thirty-five years ago. Edgar was watching her, but he didn't watch.'

'I'm sorry,' Kitty whispered.

'And now those children from the town swim there. I won't have them playing games where Lucy drowned. Let me see your face.' She seized Kitty's jaw with her bony fingers and turned her face. 'Kitty Wix. The baker's name is Wix. He came here with that teacher.'

'He's my father,' Kitty tried to say, but the old woman's nails dug into her cheeks. She shook Kitty's head.

'What have you stolen?'

'Nothing.'

'How did you get into my house? I won't have it. I won't have you town children here.' Suddenly she shrieked, 'Edgar!' She stood up and dragged Kitty by her wrist. 'Edgar!' She pulled her to the door with wiry strength and opened it. Again she called her son. The name seemed to rattle in the hall.

'Never here when I want him.'

'Let me go,' Kitty cried. She tried to fight, but Mrs. Marwick slapped her about the face, stinging slaps that made Kitty gasp. She pulled her down the hall to a cupboard at the end and unbolted the door. The inside was bare except for old shoes. Balls of dust ran into the hall like grey spiders.

'That's where naughty children go.'

'No!' Kitty cried, but Mrs. Marwick bundled her in. She stood in the hall, elongated, towering. Her face swelled as she leaned at Kitty, tumbled in the back.

'And they never come out.'

She slammed the door and bolted it. Kitty was locked in the dark.

◆

Irene waited until Marwick stopped chasing Noel and Phil. He was two fences back. He leaned on a gate and she imagined she could hear him panting. 'I'll get you,' he yelled.

Irene ran out of the scrub and joined the boys. 'The pin got stuck. I couldn't get it out.'

'Doesn't matter. We've got him.'

'We found rags and benzine in the barn. He trapped us but we got out through a loose board at the back. Where's Kitty?'

'She went into the house. I thought she must have come out the other side.'

'We didn't see her.' They looked back over the paddocks. Marwick was trudging away, hands on hips, on a line that would take him across the old croquet lawn to the house.

'If he gets her, he'll kill her,' Noel said.

'Maybe she's hidden,' Phil said.

'How's she going to get out?'

'Let's get the police,' Irene cried. They looked at each other. Things had got beyond them. Edgar Marwick didn't know any rules. He was like something springing out of nightmares into life.

They ran all the way into town and told their story to Sergeant McCaa. He looked at them sourly. 'A real bunch of Hottentots, aren't you? All right, come on.'

He put them in his car and drove out over the river bridge, round the foot of Settlers Hill, and along the road through the scrub to Marwick's farm. 'This had better be true.'

Thomas Hedges heard the car cross the one-way bridge. He was collecting river-bugs on a tranquil stretch above Girlie's Hole. He had his specimen case and magnifying glass and a tiny muslin net, and was inspecting a boatman on the tip of his index finger when he heard the Gatling-gun rattle of boards and saw the car, with Irene Chalmers sitting by McCaa, and Phil and Noel in the back. He packed up quickly, left his case under the bridge, and set out for the farm.

In the yard Edgar Marwick stopped the grinding wheel. He had gone back to sharpening the sickle and held it in his hand as McCaa came up with the children. He felt the edge with his thumb and looked at Noel and Phil with a white-toothed grin.

'So, you caught them?'

'They came to me, Mr. Marwick,' McCaa said.

'What's their story this time?'

109

'Where's my sister?' Noel burst out.

'What?' Edgar Marwick said. To McCaa he said, 'Who's he talking about?'

'There were four of them. Another girl.'

Marwick shook his head. 'I only saw these two. Sniffing round in my barn. What'd you pinch? Have you turned their pockets out?' he asked McCaa.

'What have you done with her?' Noel cried.

McCaa put his hand on his shoulder. 'One thing at a time. I'd like to look in your barn, Mr. Marwick.'

'What for?'

'They say you've got benzine in there.'

'They're still on that? All right, go ahead. But it better be the last time I see these kids. I'm tired of it.'

They all went into the barn, Marwick last, and Phil led them round the hay pile to the door. It was closed and bolted. Hay was piled in front of it again. He swept it aside with a sick feeling. He knew what he would find. And the rags and benzine were gone. All the little room contained was a pile of empty sacks and a length of rusty chain. Noel and McCaa looked over his shoulder.

'It was there,' Noel cried. 'Three or four cans. And some rags.'

'He's shifted it,' Phil said.

Marwick said nothing.

'Outside,' McCaa said to the boys. He pushed them ahead of him into the yard.

'Told you it was moonshine,' Marwick said. 'That place has been empty since I put the hay in.'

Thomas Hedges arrived. 'What's going on?'

'Keep out of this, Mr. Hedges,' McCaa said.

'And get off my property,' Marwick said.

'We found rags and benzine in his barn,' Phil cried.

'He's shifted it. And he's got Kitty.'

Marwick said to McCaa, 'I've had enough of this. I want you to charge these children with trespassing in my barn. And they jammed my pump.' He took the hairpin out of his pocket and showed it to the sergeant. 'Stuck in the valve.'

McCaa took it. His mouth grew thin. 'Yours?' he asked Irene.

'Yes,' she said in a voice almost too small to be heard.

'Did you jam the pump?'

'Yes.'

'I showed her how. So we could search the barn,' Phil said.

McCaa ignored him. 'I suppose you're the one who wrote that letter?'

'Yes, Sir.'

'Britannia. Who's Belgium?'

'I'm Belgium.'

'My sister's Britannia,' Noel burst out. 'And he's done something to her.'

'What about this other girl, Mr. Marwick?' McCaa said.

A voice called imperiously from the veranda, 'If you're looking for the Wix girl, she's in here.' Mrs. Marwick stood by the half-open door. She held her stick and turned it in her hand, pointing down the hall. Then she pushed the door with it, swinging it wide. 'And I'll be pleased if she's taken away.' She went into the hall.

McCaa, the children and Hedges trooped after her. Marwick came last. She led them under the chandeliers, along the floral carpet strip, and came to a cupboard built in a wall. She hooked back the bolt with a white forefinger and threw the door open dramatically. Kitty sat against the back wall, crouching like a monkey in a den. Her face was white as paper. She blinked in the light.

Hedges pushed between the sergeant and Mrs. Marwick. He took Kitty's arms and lifted her out. Noel came and put his arm around her.

Hedges swung round. 'Who did this? You?' To Marwick.

'It was me, Mr. Hedges,' Mrs. Marwick said. 'I caught her stealing things in my parlor.'

They looked at Kitty. Her face was taking color. She licked her lips, then spoke in a pale little voice. 'I wasn't stealing.' She fumbled at her blouse with fingers that seemed numb, undid a button. She pulled out the red balaclava and held it up.

'Only this.'

CHAPTER NINE

The Moon,
and Other Things...

THE CHANDELIERS TINKLED in a breeze coming through the door. From its pen by the barn the Jersey bull gave a bellow as though announcing some important event. McCaa stepped forward and took the balaclava from Kitty's fingers. He turned to Edgar Marwick.

'Mr. Marwick?'

Marwick blinked. He shook his head. 'I've never seen it.' He swallowed and his Adam's apple travelled up his throat and down again. 'We've only got this girl's word she saw someone in a balaclava.'

'And ours,' Phil said.

McCaa turned to Kitty. 'Where did you find it?'

'In there.' Kitty pointed. 'In that room.'

Mrs. Marwick moved for the first time since she had opened the cupboard. She pushed the door with her stick and rammed in the bolt. 'The child's telling lies.'

'No,' Kitty said. 'It was in the piano.' McCaa looked at her with disbelief. 'Inside,' she said, 'down in the wires. I played a note and it made no sound, so I had a look.'

'I've never heard such rubbish. Balaclavas in pianos. She's making it up,' Mrs. Marwick said.

'I'm not.'

'We'll have pots and pans in the bathtub next.' But she found McCaa still watching her. She snatched the balaclava from his fingers and held it under her son's nose. 'Is this yours?'

'No, it's not.'

'There! You see?'

McCaa took the garment back. This time he held it in his fist. He took no more notice of Mrs. Marwick, but said to Edgar, 'And that overcoat I asked you about? No buttons.'

'Not mine either. If you ask me, these boys found that thing.' He flicked at the balaclava with his forefinger. 'Or stole it somewhere and came here to hide it, to make trouble. This schoolteacher's probably in it too. He's been sneaking about on my land.'

'I've been collecting specimens in a public river,' Hedges said. He sounded pompous.

'All right. All right,' McCaa said. He showed the balaclava to Mrs. Marwick. 'You've never seen it, ma'am?'

'Certainly not.'

'Or you?' To Edgar.

'No, I haven't.'

McCaa turned to Kitty. 'And you, young lady? You stick to your story?'

'It was in the piano.' Mrs. Marwick glared at her but Kitty looked back steadily. She felt safe with Hedges behind her.

McCaa put the balaclava in his pocket. 'Well, I'll keep it. I'll make some inquiries. I think you children better go home now. Unless you want to press that charge, Mr. Marwick?'

Mrs. Marwick answered for him, 'No, we don't. Just keep them off my land. And out of my house.'

'And away from my pump,' Edgar Marwick said, but he spoke as though his mother prompted him. Thomas Hedges noticed that his eyes rested, with an expression almost of grieving, on the lump made by the balaclava in McCaa's jacket pocket.

They went down the hall and across the veranda and the door banged shut behind them. McCaa gave a curt nod and went off to look in the barn again.

'He won't find anything,' Noel said.

They walked along the road to the bridge. Phil climbed down the bank and retrieved Hedges' specimen case.

'It's him, isn't it, Sir? Mr. Marwick?'

'Yes, it's him.'

'He couldn't have put that benzine far away. We could go back — '

'No,' Hedges said. 'He's dangerous. Stay away.'

McCaa's car went by and left them in a cloud of dust.

'You leave it to Sergeant McCaa. He's no fool. He'll keep an eye on Marwick. I don't think there'll be any more fires.'

'Will he tell on us?' Irene said. 'About the pump?'

'I don't think so. He's more concerned with Marwick right now.'

'If my mother finds out she'll send me away from Jessop. I'll pretend I've got asthma.'

'I'll pretend I didn't hear that,' Hedges said. 'Kitty? You all right?'

'Yes,' Kitty said.

'You did very well. How did you manage in that cupboard?'

Kitty smiled. Her color had come back. In fact, the world seemed more brightly colored than it had been before she was locked in the dark. The breeze touched her skin as though a layer was gone, the sound of the river, bubbling on its stones, ran into the inside of her head as though water itself were running there. Mrs. Marwick, the dusty room, the child in the photographs, thinned and slipped away until she could hardly recall them.

'Do you remember,' she said, 'you told us about a man in prison for years, and he recited all the poems he knew, all the long ones . . . ?'

'*Paradise Lost.*'

'Yes. So he didn't seem to be in prison at all. Well, I closed my eyes and I went over all my Britannia speeches.'

Hedges laughed. They had never heard him laugh so heartily. 'Three cheers for Mrs. Bolton!' he shouted.

They crossed the footbridge and turned up Leckie's Lane. They said goodbye and Noel and Kitty and Irene turned in at the Wix gate and went inside. Mrs. Wix was in the kitchen, and Noel, scenting trouble, went straight through the house and into the garden, where he tried to look as if he'd been weeding all morning. Kitty and Irene faced Mrs. Wix. She was still knitting socks for the Belgian Relief Fund, and dropping stitches, and berating the needles and the wool, and herself. She had a strong sense that she would be better employed milking cows or shoeing horses. Kitty and Irene, grimy-kneed and guilty-faced, gave her something to focus her anger on. She listened to their story, and said, 'The pair of you deserve a jolly good hiding. But you, Miss — ' to Irene — 'I suppose you never get touched?'

'Mum hits my knuckles with a pencil,' Irene said. 'It hurts,' she added, as Kitty sniggered.

Mrs. Wix knitted ferociously. 'It's the willow stick for you,' she said to Kitty. 'And that brother of yours. He needn't think he can hide in the garden.'

'I've already been locked in a cupboard,' Kitty complained.

'It serves you right.'

'She said I'd never get out.'

'Did she? I would have had a word to say about that.'

'She thought I was her daughter. She made me play the piano. It should have been you,' she said to Irene.

'She doesn't have a daughter,' Mrs. Wix said.

'Lucy. She was drowned.'

Mrs. Wix lowered her knitting. 'That's right. Lucy Marwick. My mother used to talk about her. It happened on the same day she was married.'

'What happened?'

'She was drowned in Girlie's Hole. Where you swim. Her brother was supposed to be watching her, but he went off fishing with some friends. She must have slipped in the rapids. They found her in the big pool, down at the bottom.'

'There's photos of her everywhere. On the mantelpiece and on the piano. She was pretty.'

'Very spoiled my mother said. She used to see her in town with her mother, always sucking sweets, and dressed up to the nines.' Mrs. Wix looked at Irene as though there were a lesson for her in this. Then she relented. 'Still, it wasn't her fault. Her mother was a very social woman. And her father now, he ran for mayor. They had garden parties out there. And a duke and duchess to stay, and they had that bridge built specially for the carriage. That all stopped though, after Lucy drowned. No one saw Mrs. Marwick again. She turned all her friends away. And her husband, he was just a sort of shadow of himself, my mother said. He gave up his business, gave up everything, and he soon died.'

'That's awful,' Kitty said. 'The poor people. Poor Mrs. Marwick.'

Mrs. Wix started knitting again. 'She doesn't deserve to have a bunch of wild things like you running about.' She looked at Irene. 'It's time you weren't here, Miss. Wait on.' She took a pin from her hair and pinned up Irene's where it had fallen loose at one side. 'We can't send you home looking like a haystack. As for you — ' to Kitty — 'get out into the garden and do some weeding and maybe I'll forget to tell your father.'

But Kitty went to her bedroom instead. She lay on her bed and thought of Mrs. Marwick in fine dresses, at garden parties, and thought of her now, in the parlor with the photographs everywhere and the yellow scales on the piano, and felt very sad, and frightened too, at the danger and dreadfulness of life, and the mystery of time passing by and making things old, and things that happened long ago staying alive and turning people into different shapes. And she thought of Lucy Marwick drowning. Her eyes grew hot and moist, and though tears would not roll on her cheeks, later on she counted it as crying.

◆

Hedges and Phil had turned back to look at the telescopes in the observatory. They let themselves through the iron gate and approached the little building on top of the hill.

Hedges got a key from under a brick and opened the door. The inside was almost bare — just a wooden table and wooden chair, and a cabinet for charts and the telescope on its stand, angled at the ceiling as if, Phil thought, someone had been searching for flies and spiders up there. The inside of the dome was like a skull, and the thought of spiders in it made Phil shiver, made his skin prickle. Hedges smiled at him and seemed to understand. 'It's like a big head, isn't it? And we're the brains inside. And this' — he patted the telescope — 'is our eyes.' He ran his hand down it. 'An optic nerve. It's my ambition to find a comet. Or a new planet, although I don't think there's any left.'

'And call it after yourself, Sir?'

Hedges turned sharply, but saw Phil was not being sarcastic. 'I'm not important enough,' he said, 'to be floating around in the heavens.' He spun an iron wheel and a slit opened in the roof. 'There. The eye comes open after sleep. You can come one night. I'll show you the stars.'

'Can't we look at something now?'

'There's a moon up there. But night's the best time. Still, we'll give it a go.' He unfastened a bolt and pushed a handle and the dome of the building began to move, running on a track fixed in the wall. Again Phil had the prickly feeling. It was as if someone was twisting his head on his shoulders. The slit came round from the west and faced north-east.

'Half a moon. That should be enough.' Hedges adjusted the telescope and lined it up. 'All right. Have a look.'

Phil put his eye to the eyepiece and a huge half moon sprang into view, pale as marble and smudged with grey. He gave a grunt of surprise, then drew his breath in at the closeness of it. It seemed he need only put up his arm to embrace it like a football. Then it became strange, almost terrifying. Its size was overwhelming, and a weight seemed to crush on him. Many times he'd seen the moon, full, swollen, yellow as a poorman's orange, rising over the hills, and that had not made him afraid. He felt there might be things up there watching him.

'Those are craters, Phil. Made by meteorites. Some of them are hundreds of miles across.'

'Do you think there's anyone up there, Sir?'

Hedges laughed. 'No men in the moon. Lichens maybe. Plants maybe. Micro-organisms. But nothing that needs to breathe. There's no atmosphere.'

He left Phil at the telescope for another ten minutes. Soon the boy began asking sensible questions. Drawing him away at last, Hedges said, 'You can come up at night. I'll show you Mars. And Venus. Planet of war, planet of mystery and love. Roman names, Phil. I'll lend you a book. Although I prefer Greek myself. Orpheus. That's what I'd call my new planet. When you look up there at night' — he gestured at the sky — 'you can hear a kind of harmony.' He began to close the slit.

Phil went to the table. He picked up a smaller telescope lying on some charts. 'Can I look through this?'

'Yes. Open that window.'

Phil opened a small window in the fixed part of the wall and poked out the telescope. He pointed it up the valley, focussed it, and at once, as startling as the moon, Edgar Marwick sprang into view. He was coming from the door of the farmhouse on to the veranda, carrying something. Phil saw it was a tray with a white cloth over it. Then Mrs. Marwick was in the picture. Although sitting down, she seemed to creep in from the side. She was in her wicker chair, with her wide-brimmed hat on her head, and under it, because the sun was strong, an old green tennis sun-visor. Her stick leaned on her knee. Marwick approached her. He put the tray on a wicker table and whisked off the cloth. Phil could not see what sort of food he had brought, but saw a teapot, and watched as Marwick poured tea. He felt he was hiding just out of the picture, at the veranda's edge, watching them.

'That's a good telescope, that one,' Hedges said.

'Yes.'

'What are you looking at?'

'The Marwicks.' Edgar Marwick lifted a lump of sugar with silver tongs and put it in his mother's tea. 'He's waiting on her. Like a servant.'

'She's an old lady. Maybe he's just being a good son.'

'He's giving her sandwiches. Beetroot, that's what it is. It looks like blood.'

Hedges took the telescope. 'You'll learn more up there,' he said, pointing at the sky, 'than spying down there. Close the window.'

Phil had a last look at the Marwicks, tiny figures on the veranda of a distant house, and pulled the window shut and closed the latch. Hedges put the telescope on the table.

'Does that one work at night-time too?' Phil asked.

'That's what it's for. As long as there's a light source. It's the light that makes the image, not the telescope. That just brings it close.'

They locked the observatory and hid the key and walked down to the town. Phil was still excited — by the moon, by the Marwicks? He did not know.

'I'd like to be an astronomer, Sir.'

'Perhaps you will. There are all sorts of universes, Phil. Little Irene Chalmers wants to explore one with her piano.'

Phil didn't like that comparison. His excitement was of another sort, and letting Irene Chalmers in made it ordinary. He walked by Hedges' side, disappointed, and thought of beetroot sandwiches and started feeling hungry. There wasn't much at home for lunch. He wished he'd stuck with Noel Wix. He might have got another pie.

Hedges turned with him towards the town center. 'I'm going your way. To Frau Stauffel's.'

'The piano teacher?'

'You sound surprised.'

'No, Sir.'

'Because she's a German? And I'm going to lunch with her?'

'We're fighting the Germans, Sir.'

'And you think because of that I should hate this lady?'

'If she's German.'

'Then she'll hate me. And we'll have a little war here in Jessop, to go with the big one overseas. We can do without that, Phil, don't you think?'

Phil didn't answer. He thought Hedges was just being tricky. He knew sometimes why people didn't like him.

They came to Frau Stauffel's gate. She was working in her garden, but came to Hedges, pulling off her gloves, and shook his hand.

'Frau Stauffel, this young fellow is Phil Miller.'

Phil said hello awkwardly, shuffling his feet. 'I've got to go, Sir.'

'Yes, on your way.' Hedges watched him run off. 'He's a good boy, but not sure he should talk to Germans.'

Frau Stauffel took his hand again and pulled him through the gate. 'Will you see something, Thomas?' She led him to the front door. There, crudely lettered in red paint, were the words 'Dirty Hun'.

Hedges sighed. 'When did it happen?'

'Last night.'

'Well, my dear, it could be worse. It looks like a bit of ya-hoo stuff to me. Young fellows. I'll paint it off. You'll be all right as long as the men don't start. Come inside now. Play me some music. That's the right answer for this sort of thing.'

They went inside and left the words, crooked, red, shining on the door.

CHAPTER TEN

Britannia Meets the Kaiser

MRS. BOLTON CAME to the cast of the pageant under the lime trees, holding a letter in her hands.

'Children! Children! Listen. Stop that, Miller.' (Noel was jabbing Phil's behind with the spike of his Prussian helmet.) 'Now, listen, I've had a letter from Mr. Jobling. He's coming next week. That's a whole week early. And so we've got to do the pageant then. That means practice and practice. And boys, you've got the sets to build. Girls, you must sew and sew. I've asked Mr. Hedges to let you off classes.'

'We can't learn it all in a week, Mrs. Bolton.'

'Can't is a word I don't know, Wix. I'm sure Irene knows her part already.'

'She hasn't got as many words as me,' Phil said.

'Believe me, Miller, I'd give someone else your part if there was time. Now, boys over to the trade school. And girls to the sewing room. And remember, we're not doing this for ourselves.'

'We're doing it for Bolters,' Irene whispered.

They went off to their work, and built and sewed: costumes

for Britannia and Belgium, India, Egypt; wooden rifles, a wooden trident and a wooden shield, and panels for the scenery to be painted on. They practiced their lines morning and afternoon, and learned their songs and movements, and had only two or three lessons a day — arithmetic and English. The dress rehearsal went off without too many mistakes. In spite of Mrs. Bolton, the children enjoyed themselves.

On the day of the pageant, Thomas Hedges told them to forget about it until they actually climbed on the stage. 'There's just one thing. Some of you are still not speaking properly. You have to throw your voice at the back of the room. Choose someone back there and throw it at him like a cricket ball.'

'What if he drops it, Sir?'

'Very funny, Wix. Phil, you need to open your mouth. The voice-box, the tongue, the lips, they're a musical instrument. Think of a trumpet. Think of a grand piano.'

'Is the voice-box really shaped like a box?' Kitty said.

'No, it's more like a harp, and like the bagpipes.' He seized a stick of chalk and drew larynx and vocal cords on the blackboard and told them how the cords were tightened or loosened and how different sounds were made by forcing air through them.

'Can you see that on a skeleton, Sir?'

'No, it's cartilage. It doesn't last.'

'Can we see Miss Perez?'

'Not today.'

'Those bumps you were telling us about on people's heads?'

'Yes, Kitty. Do you remember the word?'

'Phrenology. When someone like the fire-raiser stops lighting fires, do his bumps go down?'

'He hasn't stopped,' Bob Taylor cried. 'He'll light some more, I bet.'

'Well then, Miller and Wix can put them out,' Hedges said. 'But no, Kitty, to answer your question. Phrenology is just mumbo-jumbo. People's heads don't change shape. And the fire-raiser doesn't have special bumps.'

'Beethoven had a big head, Sir,' Irene said.

'Beethoven was a German,' Melva Dyer said.

'Sir,' Ray Stack cried, 'that town the Russians captured. How do you say it?'

'This one?' Hedges wrote 'Przemysl' on the blackboard. 'I don't know. But it's here.' He pointed it out on the map. 'Important because it's on a river.'

'The Russians are bombarding the Bosphorous, Sir,' Phil said.

'Sir, when we fight again, will it be the Germans or the Turks?' Noel asked.

'I don't know. The Turks, I think.'

'They're no good,' Ray Stack said. 'We beat them easy in Egypt.'

'Some of you boys,' Hedges said, 'seem to think it's a game. Men are dying out there. Thousands of them. All because we haven't got control of what's in here.' He tapped his skull, but saw they did not understand. 'Well,' he said, 'you can make fine speeches about it tonight for Mr. Jobling. For the moment we'd better do some arithmetic.' And he started writing sums on the board. Yes, he thought, Beethoven was a German, and so was Bismark, and so's the Kaiser. And Shakespeare was English, but so was Butcher

Cumberland. He wasn't sure he understood himself. Was there any chance these children would make sense of it one day?

◆

St Andrews Hall stood next to the church. It was a narrow, tall-roofed building of weatherboard, and it stood behind a wrought-iron fence and a strip of lawn. In the dusk it had a yellow glow, quickly fading. Over the box-like entrance a banner made clapping sounds in the breeze. TONIGHT. PATRIOTIC PAGEANT BY THE CHILDREN OF JESSOP MAIN SCHOOL. PROCEEDS TO THE BELGIAN RELIEF FUND.

Noel and Kitty, with their costumes over their arms, came down the street and hurried inside. They went up the central aisle, through chairs and benches for 200 people, and climbed the steps to the stage, hearing a clatter and buzz behind the curtains. Mrs. Bolton was helping boys place backdrops painted on panels. The center one showed green fields, red poppies, yellow cows: the fields of Belgium. On the left were the white cliffs of Dover, with blue sky and a little church. On the right a forest of dark trees was bending in a storm. Clouds like grey pumpkins rolled in the sky, where black crows with open beaks were flying. Noel, in his part of Kaiser, grinned with satisfaction. His backdrop was best.

Irene, in peasant skirt and cap and blouse, ran up to Kitty. 'How do I look?'

'Marvelous.'

'Hurry and get changed, Kitty. I want to look at you,' Mrs. Bolton said. Her face was so damp and anxious, Kitty felt sorry for her. 'Yes, Mrs. Bolton.' She went to the changing room, past India and Egypt looking so strange and beautiful she began to regret her own plain costume, and the drum and fife boys in their belts and glengarries. Noel went to the boys' changing room and found a place in a corner. He could scarcely move for Canada, Australia, Hun soldiers and a Ghurka and a Turk, and Wipaki in a grass skirt, with a spear. Phil had not arrived yet. 'He'll be late,' Bob Taylor said with satisfaction; and out on the stage Mrs. Bolton was crying, 'I knew I should never have trusted that boy.'

Irene, looking through the curtain, said, 'Here he is, Mrs. Bolton.'

Phil came up the steps on to the stage. He had his costume wrapped in newspaper, and a pair of shoes on his feet tonight. Mrs. Bolton ran at him and slapped his head.

'You're late. Where have you been? Mr. Jobling's here.'

'There's plenty of time — '

'Don't answer me back. Go and change. Oh, look at your shoes. Absolutely filthy. One of you boys in the band, change with him. Quick, get them off. We can't have New Zealand in dirty shoes.' She pushed Phil away by the nape of his neck.

Kitty came back and joined Irene. They peered through a crack in the curtains. The hall was almost half full and more people were coming in every moment. Kitty was wearing a long white robe and a plumed Roman helmet, which she took off to see better through the crack.

'There's my mum and dad. Where are yours?'

'Coming in now. With Mr. Jobling.'

'Isn't he fat?'

'His feet smell. It's true. He took his shoes off under our

128

table. And he touched Nancy on her bottom. She says she's going to leave and get a job in a factory.'

'He's got a face like huhu grubs. I wonder where Mr. Hedges is.'

'Perhaps he's not coming.'

Hedges was in Frau Stauffel's parlor. He turned away from the French doors and let the curtains fall. 'Jobling's gone in. I'll have to get along there now, Lotte.' He took her hands. 'You'll be all right. A lot of jingoistic huff and puff and then it's over. Keep your curtains closed.' He went back to the door and pulled the folds more tightly together. 'Have an early night. I'll come by. I'll see there's no more painting.'

'Stones on my roof too, last night.'

'Lotte, there's an answer to all this.' He tried to take her hands again, but she drew them away.

'I can't bring my worries to you, Thomas. What a dowry.'

'I'm good at worries. And besides, you'd bring other things.'

'I know. I will think.' She patted his lapels. 'You must go. To your huff and puff.'

As he went along to the hall, he had a premonition it would be more than that. Some young fellows were lounging and smoking by the door. He knew them. It was only four or five years since they'd been giving him trouble in his classroom. He went in and took his place by Jobling and Mr. and Mrs. Chalmers in the front row. Jobling beamed at him with his red, clever face — it was, all the same, a stupid face — and said in his plummy voice, 'Nearly late, Mr. Hedges. I'd have had to give you six of the best.'

'Then you'd have lost my vote, Mr. Jobling,' Hedges said,

and saw the politician narrow his eyes. The fool had never had his vote, and knew it very well.

On the stage, Mrs. Bolton was spinning like a top. 'You drum and fife boys, where are you? Who's missing? Hankin, wipe your nose. Not on your sleeve, boy. Hun, you get in the wings. You can't be on for the National Anthem.' She gave Noel a push. 'Off you go with him, Turk. And be ready for your cue.' She pushed the Turk — in turban, baggy trousers, huge moustache — then ran at Kitty, still peering through the curtains. 'Kitty, Kitty, over here with your Britannic group. Get on your throne. Where's your trident? Where's your shield?'

'Here, Mrs. Bolton,' Kitty said, taking them from behind the throne. The shield had a Union Jack painted on it and the trident was white with silver prongs. She mounted her high throne and sat down. Then, as if by magic, things were ready. The band and choir were at the back, Britannia and her empire and her allies center stage, Kaiser, Turk, and Prussian squad in the wings, and boys waiting on the curtain ropes. Mrs. Bolton dabbed her face with her handkerchief. 'Now, breathe deep. Be absolutely still, like British sentries. Are they ready?'

'Yes, Mrs. Bolton,' said a girl watching through the curtains.

Mrs. Bolton went to the piano and sat down. She signalled the boys and the curtains slid back, displaying the tableau. The audience began to clap, but she cut the sound off with a chord, the National Anthem, and everyone was on their feet and singing.

Kitty sat. It felt wrong at first, but then she liked it. She kept her head still but could see Mr. Jobling and Clippy

Hedges and Irene's mother and father, and two rows back her own; and all the singing faces, with mouths opening and closing like fish in a bowl; and over the heads a little strip of dark outside the door with cigarettes glowing in it. She wondered if Edgar Marwick was in the audience.

Marwick was over the road, outside the hall. He had not meant to come to town that night. Since Sergeant McCaa's visit he had not moved off the farm. He grieved for the loss of his balaclava. It was as if part of his body had been cut off, and though he dreamed of fires, he could no longer feel the heat of flames.

He had worked hard. He had cleared a whole hillside of scrub in the past week. In the afternoon he had walked down with his axe, past Buck's Hole, and stopped to look at it, thinking of Hedges and the boys. Suddenly he had seen the way the tree he was standing by would fall if he chopped it down. Straight in. Straight in Buck's Hole. That would finish it. That would be the end of all their swimming. He gave a whoop, and punched the tree with the heel of his axe, and lined it up and started chopping. He made a notch, and cut a clean 'V' in the other side, breathing through his nose, feeling the warm trickle of sweat on his chest. But before he was through, the axe broke at the head and he was left holding the haft. He could not believe it. Everything was against him. He hurled the haft into Buck's Hole, and pushed the tree with all his body's weight, but although it was almost cut through, it would not fall. Marwick gave a shout of rage, then he almost cried like a boy. He trudged back to the house and splashed water on his face from the tap on the tank stand. Well, he thought, I'll take the other axe. I'll go back there. I'll do it in the morning.

When he went into the house he heard his mother playing the piano. The sound came down the hall like the scratching of possum claws on an iron roof. He was insulted, injured by it, this journey she made into a past where he was at fault. Lucy? Who was Lucy? He no longer remembered her face. All he remembered was being locked in the dark.

He strode down the hall and threw open the door. She was at the yellow keys, as though plucking bones from a fish.

'Go away, Edgar. You shouldn't come in here. Go away.'

'She's been dead thirty-five years. She's not coming back.'

'She came. She played for me.'

'That was the Wix girl. I should clear out all this junk.' He crossed the room and seized the curtains.

'No! No light!' she cried in a terrible voice.

He shook the curtains, slapped them with the back of his fist. Dust sprang out and clouded around his face. He retreated from it. 'You're loony, Ma. You should be put away.'

'Get out of Lucy's room.'

'I'll get out. You think I want to stay? You think I want to be here with you?' He passed the piano and gave it a punch that tumbled the scales off the stand. A scratchy complaint came from inside. 'I should smash that thing. I should use it for firewood.' He opened the door.

'Edgar!' As always, that cry stopped him in his tracks. 'Don't speak to me in that way. And never come into this room again. Now go away.'

He slammed the door and went to the kitchen. He looked for food but there was none. The sound of the piano came through the house. It tangled in his head like wire. He ran to his room, tore off his clothes and put on clean ones.

He left the house and headed down the road and over the bridge, not knowing where he was going. Once he ran his hand over his scalp, but the balaclava was not there. He did not feel alive. No fire was burning in his head.

A meal in a restaurant made him feel better. He sat sucking meat shreds from his teeth, and thought of his mother, and wondered what he would do when she died. He did not want that. He wanted to live forever on the farm and look after her. But she was old, she would die soon. And she was crazy. Tears came into his eyes as he thought of her playing Lucy's piano.

Edgar Marwick left the restaurant and walked through the town. He heard people singing and stopped outside a hall. The song was the National Anthem and he stood at attention until it was over, thinking how well the hall would burn, but not thinking seriously of it. He was not angry now, but sad. When the singing stopped, he went through the iron gate and paid his shilling and went into the hall. It was full. He stood against the wall at the back and watched costumed children on a stage. They were saying speeches and he began to smile, enjoying it.

Kitty saw him come in. High on her throne, regal posed — 'chin up, eyes front' — she had a clear sight of the door. Edgar Marwick stood there a moment, then slid along the wall, under Sunday-School texts hanging from nails, and stood with arms folded, looking at her. She felt as if the hall had grown cold, and no one else was there, just her and this man. She rolled her eyes, looking for Noel, but he was at the side of the stage, shouting at Irene. Phil was behind her throne with the other Dominions. She heard him whisper, 'Marwick,' close to her ear. It made her feel better. No one could get them on this stage. She saw Clippy Hedges, and two rows back her mother and father, with grins on their faces as they listened to Noel. Edgar Marwick became indistinct at the back of the hall. She began to think of her first speech. It was not far away.

Irene knelt at Noel's feet with her hands clasped under her chin. Helmeted, grey-uniformed, he faced her, grinning fiercely. He loved the lines he had to say. He screwed his hands as though wringing the neck of a bird; he stamped his foot as though squashing caterpillars. 'I shall tear this poppy Belgium from her stem. My heel shall grind her petals in the mud.'

Irene ran to Kitty's throne and knelt at her feet. 'O Britannia, Britannia. Pity our distress. The imperious Kaiser marches his German horde across our plains to carry death. See how the black clouds roll. See how the war birds gather in the north. Help us, O great neighbor. Fair Britannia, help us now!'

Kitty heard drums roll behind her. She heard a ragged fanfare of trumpets. Softly she said, 'Poor little Belgium, brave but powerless against the foe.' She raised her voice. 'Shall she be trampled underfoot while we stand by neglectful of our pledge? And France, great France, grown closer in our friendship recently. She has not caused this war. She cries for help.'

'Oh, help! Oh, help!' France cried.

Kitty stood up. 'We hear the call!' She stamped the heel of her trident on the floor. 'Oh, fight we must and fight we will. Who will follow? Sons and daughters, speak!'

Canada stepped from behind the throne. 'I will follow.'

Australia stepped forward. 'I.'

India. 'And I.'

Phil came two paces out, dressed in an army uniform. He

shouldered his wooden rifle and saluted Kitty. 'And I. Mother of Empire! Our New Zealand home is so far from the *white* cliffs of Old England that it might be thought we had forgot those from whom we sprung. It is not so! Furthest flung of your Empire we may be, but our character and customs are your own. We are the Britain of the South. . .'

'Bravo!' Jobling cried.

'Our men and boys are pressing to join the colors.' He faced the audience and lifted his voice.

> *Who would not fight for England?*
> *Who would not fling a life*
> *I' the ring to meet the tyrant's gage*
> *And glory in the strife?*

'Bravo!'

Mrs. Bolton struck a chord on the piano. The choir sang — and Jobling was on his feet, singing too, and the hall joined in:

> *Old England's sons are English yet,*
> *Old England's hearts are strong;*
> *And still she wears her coronet*
> *Aflame with sword and song.*
> *As in their pride our fathers died,*
> *If need be so die we . . .*

The words of the song went into the night, past the lounging youths on the lawn. At her piano, Frau Stauffel heard them distantly. She went to the curtains and drew them back and peered up the street. This, she thought, was music to swell people up and make them blind and make them silly. It did the same work as beer and rabble-rousing speeches. It pained her to think of Irene, her *wunderkind,* opening her mouth and making noises of that sort, and after a moment she went back to her piano and played for Irene a Brahms lullaby, sending it softly on its way, a message for her, an act of faith in the goodness of music. Her eyes grew damp as she played, and when it was done she closed the piano lid and sat a while with her hands on it. Then she turned out the lights and sat in a chair. The singing in the hall had stopped. That meant more speeches, she supposed, more huff and puff. She would stay here in the dark until it was over.

A mile away, Mrs. Marwick also sat in the dark, but she was sleeping. No chink of light entered the room. Her hair had tumbled down, and in her dream the touch of it on her cheeks was Lucy stroking her and the squeak of mice in the wall was Lucy's voice. She smiled and sighed and groaned in her sleep.

Flags were waving on the stage. Boasts and promises were made. 'The foeman will find neither coward nor slave, Neath the Red Cross of England the flag of the brave,' Phil declared. And one by one allies and Dominions pledged themselves. Then Kitty came down from her throne.

'Thanks, my good sons and daughters. Your warmth today does credit to your fathers and their fathers, the blood of noble Britons dead and gone. Together we stand ready. Forth we go to right this monstrous wrong.'

'Yes, yes,' the Britannic group cried. 'The British bulldog is aroused. Let him come to grips with this German bully.' They levelled their wooden rifles at Noel and the Turk.

Drums made the sound of rifle shots. The Turk fell dead. Noel sank to his knees. He gnashed his teeth and clawed his fingers, refusing to die. Kitty, with her shield on her arm, ran at him and jabbed him with her trident. He clawed at it and she jabbed him again, hard in the stomach. He howled like a monkey, and sank on his face, and died. Kitty rested the prongs of the trident on his back. The Britannic group, rifles pointing down, shot him again. Bang! Bang! Then Mrs. Bolton struck up on her piano and everyone sang *Land of Hope and Glory*. When it was over, Jobling bounded up the steps to the stage like a rubber ball.

'Friends! Friends!' The young men had come in from the street. They whistled and cheered while the audience clapped. 'Friends! People of Jessop!' Jobling stilled them with voice and hand. 'What a marvelous pageant! What a glorious night! These children, our children, they've shown us the way. Who doesn't want to go out and shoot a Hun right now? For our glorious Empire? For Mother England? Oh yes! There's a spirit abroad in our gallant land. Not just in our brave boys who go and fight, and in the mothers who give their sons. In our children. In our youth. In our old folk. Everywhere. Last month, remember, in Wellington, how they threw that German car in the harbor, and the driver too.' The young men at the back shouted and cheered. 'And Gisborne, remember Gisborne, how they smashed that German pork butcher's shop? Well, there are no pork butchers in Jessop — '

'We've got Huns,' someone shouted.

'We've got that piano teacher down the road.'

'Hold on, boys. Hold on,' Jobling cried.

'Why should she sit here getting fat?'

'We don't want any Huns in Jessop.'

'Let's show 'er the door, then.'

'Run her out of town.'

'Boys! Boys!'

Irene ran to Kitty, standing with her trident behind Jobling. 'They're going to get Frau Stauffel.'

'Why doesn't Mr. Hedges stop them?'

Hedges had gone back towards the entrance. He beckoned George Wix, and the two broke through the knot of youths in the door and went outside. Meanwhile, Mr. Chalmers had climbed on the stage. 'Listen to me. Listen!'

'Why should we, Chalmers?' That was Edgar Marwick. He spoke at last.

'Your kid goes there for lessons.'

'Not any more. But listen to me —'

'Sit down, Chalmers.'

'You're a bloody Hun-lover.'

And Edgar Marwick cried, 'Enough talking, boys. Follow me.' He went out the door, and not only the young men followed him, but older ones from the body of the hall: Bob Taylor's father, Ray Stack's father.

Kitty pulled Irene past the dressing room. 'There's a way down the back.' They went along a corridor by the back wall and out a narrow door into a yard. Kitty ran ahead, over a tennis court. Her robes glimmered in the dark. 'This way. Hurry.' They ran along a path between houses and the park. Gardens full of shadows stood in the moonlight. The playing fields were like a silver lake.

'There's no light on.'

'It doesn't matter. Inside. Quick. We'll have to wake her.'

They ran into Frau Stauffel's back garden and listened at

her kitchen door. A sound of men shouting came from up the road by the hall. In the front of the house a light went on.

'She's there. I'm going in.' Kitty tried the door. It opened. They went into the kitchen and felt their way across to another door. Then they were in the hall and light streamed from the parlor.

'Frau Stauffel,' Irene called. They ran in.

Frau Stauffel was at the French doors, holding the curtains aside. 'What? What is happening?'

'They're coming to get you. Men from the hall. Come with us.'

The noise of the mob rolled like a wave on a beach. A black wave of figures advanced in the street, filling it to the sides, with eyes and hands and teeth white like foam.

'Frau Stauffel!' Irene tried to pull her away from the doors.

'There's a man running on my path.'

The front door opened. Feet thudded in the hall. George Wix came in. 'How did you girls get here? Frau Stauffel, no time to explain. Hedges is out there, he'll try to stop them. We'll go the back way.'

'I do not understand —' A stone smashed through a glass panel in the door. *Mein Gott!*'

'Come on,' Irene screamed. She took Frau Stauffel and pulled. Wix took her other arm. Kitty ran ahead, opening doors. They went out through the kitchen into the garden, on to the path, and hurried along by the park. A sound of more glass smashing came from the cottage.

There, inside the front gate, Hedges faced the mob. Stones flew over him and thudded against the house and rattled on its roof. One struck his ribs and he felt skin tear. 'Stop!' he cried. 'You can't do this.' With their yellow eyes, panting mouths, they were like wolves in an Arctic night. Edgar Marwick kicked the gate open.

'She's your fancy lady, teacher. Out of my way.' He led the rush up the path. They knocked Hedges down and trampled on him. They burst through the front door, jamming in it, tearing at each other to go first. A baying and a yelping came from them. Hedges lay on the ground, with blood on his face. He struggled to his knees. Phil and Noel arrived, in their uniforms. 'Are you all right, Sir?'

'Yes. Stay back.'

Cries of rage came from the house. Windows burst out from inside. And Marwick's bull voice roared, 'A Hun piano!' The French doors exploded into the garden. There he stood, one arm raised, silhouetted in the light. Then he seized the curtains and tore them down and flung them backwards into the room. 'This way,' he yelled, 'bring it out.' Men heaved the piano through the door. They crashed it on its back and rolled it like a boulder in the flower beds. Hedges started forward, but Wix came panting round from the back of the house, 'They'll tear you to bits. She's safe. She's in the bakehouse with Kitty and Irene.'

Ray Stack's father came running through the house with an axe from the garden shed. He attacked the piano with it, chopping like an axeman at a fair. The black wood splintered and sprang in yellow chips. The brass letters of the name popped out, keys flew like snapped-off teeth, wires jangled. Marwick had vanished into the house. He reappeared, huge in the broken doors. He held a bottle high in his hand, as though he meant to swig from it. Then he lurched down through the flowers, broke through the yelling men, shoved Ray Stack's father aside. He tipped the bottle up and liquid ran down in a silver stream and splashed on the piano. He held the bottle until it was empty, then threw it backhanded at the house, where it smashed on the wall. He took a box of matches from his pocket and gave it a manic rattle. Then he struck one and threw it on the piano. Flames leaped up and licked him. To Noel and Phil he seemed to stand in the middle of them. His hands ran over his skull, feeling for something. Flames leaped redly in his eyes. It seemed as though the inside of his head was on fire.

CHAPTER ELEVEN

Girlie's Hole

MORNING. A bird was singing. And that, Wix thought, as he stirred the charred remains of the piano with his foot, shows there's still a bit of good sense in the world. Boards were nailed in the shape of a St. Patrick's cross over Frau Stauffel's French doors. Broken glass lay in the trampled flowers. But the thrush swelled her speckled breast and shouted happily. Wix yawned, after his shortened sleep. If he were a bird, he thought, he too would sing on this lovely morning, in spite of the human nastiness of the night.

Hedges and Sergeant McCaa came out the front door. Hedges closed it, locked it with a key.

'I gave them what-for,' McCaa was saying. 'It won't happen again.'

'As long as Jobling stays in Wellington where he belongs. Are you charging anyone?'

'That might come back on Mrs. Stauffel.'

Hedges agreed. 'Marwick was ringleader.'

'I'm keeping an eye on him. For other reasons,' McCaa said.

'He's certifiable,' Wix said.

'He knows I'm watching him. There'll be no more fires.' McCaa got in his car and drove away. Hedges and Wix strolled up the street.

'I wish I was that confident,' Hedges said. 'Lotte all right?'

'She's taking it well. She'd like to see you. She can stay as long as she likes, you know. We've got the room. Although young Irene Chalmers is coming tonight.' Wix grinned at Hedges. 'O! when degree is shaked.'

Hedges laughed, and said, 'If I know Lotte, she'll want to get back home and start cleaning up. There's something else you might help me with, though . . .' They strolled along past the hall, talking of it.

In the Wix kitchen Kitty and Noel and Frau Stauffel were eating breakfast. 'Outside in the street, *Walpurgisnacht* — Witches sabbath — but Irene and Kitty — two angels.'

'She was more like a devil with that fork,' Noel said. 'You should see the bruise on my ribs where she poked me.'

'That's enough, Noel,' Mrs. Wix said. 'More porridge, Mrs. Stauffel? There's plenty in the pot.'

'I am fat enough. You are spoiling me.' She held out her plate and Mrs. Wix ladled porridge in. 'In *München* — in Munich — where I was born, the pastry shops, the lovely *torte*. . . Perhaps I should not talk of German things?'

'It might be wise,' Mrs. Wix said.

'If there's pastry shops, Dad would like to go there,' Kitty said.

Voices sounded in the hall and Wix came in. 'I've brought Tom Hedges to see you, Mrs. Stauffel. You'll find him in there, in the sitting room.' He winked at his wife when Frau Stauffel had gone. 'Any of that porridge left for me?'

143

Kitty had finished. She excused herself and went to her bedroom, but stopped beyond the sitting-room door, which was ajar, and peered through the crack. Hedges and Frau Stauffel were by the window.

'It's not as bad as I thought,' Hedges said. 'There's things broken in the parlor. The busts.'

'Barbarians!' Frau Stauffel exclaimed.

'Mozart's all right. A chip off his ear. Beethoven's in pieces. I can't sort him out from Brahms.'

'They are the Huns. They are Visigoths.'

'The French doors are gone. And some windows broken.' Kitty saw him take Frau Stauffel's hands. 'As for the piano — I'm sorry, Lotte.'

'It does not matter. I shall buy another. They did not burn my fingers.' She freed one hand and touched the bruise on his face. 'And Thomas, now I shall marry you. Because I am not afraid. And you are not. And that is why. Today I shall go home and clean my house. For us to live in when we are *der Mann und die Frau.*'

Kitty watched, breathless, but then she felt a stinging slap on her bottom, and half an hour later, at school, it was still sore.

'She kissed him,' she told Irene.

'Where? On the cheek? On the mouth?'

'I couldn't tell. Mum caught me. She gave me a whack. It's just as well you're staying tonight or I'd get another.'

'Fancy kissing someone as ugly as Clippy.'

Hedges was approaching along the footpath. 'Good morning, Mr. Hedges.'

'Good morning, Mr. Hedges,' Kitty sang. They beamed at him.

144

'Good morning, girls.' He looked at them suspiciously and went on.

'If he marries Frau Stauffel she'll be Mrs. Hedges. I'll be able to go back for piano lessons,' Irene said.

'She'll still be German. I'll bet people will start calling him Herr Hedges.'

Meanwhile, Hedges reached the gate and stopped to talk to Phil, lounging there. 'Ah, Phil! I've had a letter from your father.'

'Yes,' Phil said. He had been expecting this.

'He's keen on college. Wants you to have a proper chance.'

Phil nodded glumly.

'As for somewhere to stay — I've been talking with Mr. and Mrs. Wix.'

'Wix?' Phil wasn't sure he liked that.

'Good people, Phil. They'll make you clean your teeth, eh?'

'How long will I stay?'

'Two or three weeks. Then I've got another idea.' He looked sly. 'I'll tell you later. Somewhere I think you'll do well.'

Probably with some parson, Phil thought, although Hedges didn't like parsons much. 'When do I go?'

'Tomorrow night. One more night in your old house, eh? Noel can help you shift.' He looked at his watch. 'Late.' He pointed. 'Bell. Go on, Phil. We'll talk later.'

Phil trotted off. Then he ran, and climbed the stairs to the belfry. He threw a glance at Miss Perez's cupboard and crossed through the jumble of buckets and desks to a tiny fixed window in the wall. He rubbed away dust with his hand and looked at Hedges talking with children in the playground. Suddenly he knew where he would be going after the Wixes, and it frightened him. He gave a groan. As if he had heard, Hedges looked up at the belfry. He pulled out his watch again. Phil jumped for the rope and gave a tug. The bell pealed out.

The classroom buzzed that morning. The children could not stop talking of the pageant and the attack on Frau Stauffel's house. The purple bruise on Clippy's cheek kept it all alive. Then Mrs. Bolton came in and Clippy stood at the window with his back to her while she talked to the class.

'Quiet! Quiet children! I know you're excited. Last night was a most unusual night, but I want to say how pleased I am with you — apart from those who were late.' She looked at Phil. 'You played your parts beautifully. Irene, you did very well. And Noel and Kitty.'

'Phil was good, Mrs. Bolton,' Noel said.

'Don't interrupt. I came to say thank you, on behalf of the Belgian Relief Fund. The evening was a very great success. I'm sure Mr. Hedges agrees with me.'

Hedges turned from the window. 'The singing was good. And some of the acting not too bad. If it hadn't been for a stupid speech from our MP — '

'Mr. Hedges!'

'A stupid speech. And then a gang of bully boys attacking a woman who had never done them any harm — '

'You can't blame patriotic feeling.'

'I blame stupidity, Mrs. Bolton, but it's done with. And you children did very well. Especially those who tried to help Frau Stauffel. Now, we've lost a lot of time in the last few weeks, and we've got swimming this afternoon so, unless you've got something you want to say, Mrs. Bolton?'

'No thank you!' She went out stiffly.

Hedges sighed. He would have more trouble with her, and probably with the Committee and the Board. They might even try to get rid of him when he married Lotte — but he felt complacent about that. He was angry, but satisfied with himself. The children though needed calming down. He made them take their books out and worked them hard for the rest of the morning.

After lunch, walking to the river, Phil told Noel about coming to live with him. They grinned at each other, both hoping it would be all right. Noel hoped someone would tell Phil to have more baths. Phil wondered if he would be able to help Mr. Wix bake pies again.

The girls turned off to Girlie's Hole. Hedges and the boys went over the bridge and up the riverbank, past the 'No Trespassing' sign lying in the blackberry, and came to Buck's Hole. At the house, Marwick watched them vanish in the scrub beyond the paddocks. He raised his arms and flexed his forearms. Since last night at the German woman's house he felt able to do things, and though the sight of Hedges and the boys angered him, he knew how to drive them off his land. He went into the house and down the hall and looked at his mother in the music room. She had been there all morning, talking with Lucy, and once he had heard her cry, 'Don't hide from me!', but now she sat on the sofa with her eyes closed and a photo of Lucy in her lap.

'Ma,' he said, 'you all right?'

She opened her eyes and looked at him. 'Yes, Edgar, I'm all right,' she said tiredly.

'Those town kids are here again. In the river.'

'River?'

'Don't worry about it, Ma. I'll get rid of them. You stay

here.' He closed the door. His footsteps went away down the hall.

'River?' She stood up. The photo slid from her lap and fell on the floor, cracking the glass. She looked at it. Lucy's face was dislocated. It trembled and sank; it was under water. Mrs. Marwick gave a loud cry.

Outside, Marwick strode through the yard. Axe, he thought, but then he caught sight of the crosscut saw lying across a pile of cut wood by the sawhorse. He changed course and picked it up without breaking stride and set off for the bush by the river.

Hedges had tested the water. He called out the temperature and put his thermometer away. It was cold today. This might be the last swim of the season. 'Boys for practice stroking, come with me, up on the grass. All you others in, and no horseplay.' He led the non-swimmers up the bank. 'All right, on your tummies. Point your toes. What's the matter, Hankin?'

'There's ants here, Sir.'

'Well shift somewhere else.'

'Ow, there's thistles.'

Hedges gave them a bit of time. The ones in the pool were skylarking in spite of his order, but there was no point in expecting boys not to break the rules. He was more concerned to see they didn't drown. He shouted at Phil to stop ducking people, then he turned back to the boys on the grass. But before he could start them stroking, he heard the rasp of a saw close at hand. He was so aware of Marwick, and the threat of Marwick, that he knew at once it had to do with him. He ran to the shingle.

'Quiet, boys.'

Their yelling stopped. The saw kept on, chuffing like a

train. He spotted Marwick then, half hidden in scrub, with his arms moving back and forth. A shaking started in the head of the giant matai tree over the pool.

'Marwick!' he yelled. Then saw there was no time for argument.

'Out! Run! This way!' he yelled at the boys. 'Out of the pool!'

They scattered like chickens. A loud crack came from the tree, and Marwick cried, 'Ha!'

Hedges ran into the water to his waist. He grabbed a boy, the last of them, and dragged him out by his shoulder. The tree was falling. It blotted out the sky as it came down. Its head whacked the water and seemed to empty the pool. A wave two feet high washed over the shingle and sheets of water lashed at head and chest — but the boys were out. Hedges was out. He felt the top thin branch of the tree sting his heel. Then there was only the lapping of waves in the pool.

Hedges pulled the boy to his feet. 'Nothing broken?'

'No, Sir.' He was white and shivering.

'Get dressed.'

Noel and Phil ran up. 'Are you all right, Sir?'

'I'm all right. Get them all dressed. Back to school. Wait in the playground.'

'What are you going to do, Sir?'

'It's time I had a word with Mr. Marwick.'

'He's gone mad, Sir.'

'Back to school.' The boy was right, and George Wix was right: Edgar Marwick was certifiable. Hedges knew he should not go near him, but his own anger was too great for him to be sensible. He left the boys and went through the scrub and climbed the fence. He saw Marwick walking to his house, then leaning on the gate to the croquet lawn. He rolled a cigarette as Hedges approached, put it in his mouth and struck a match. The flame burnt down to his fingers. At the last moment he lit his cigarette.

Hedges climbed another fence. He passed a patch of gorse in a hollow and came to Marwick at the lawn. Ten feet away, he stopped. Marwick did nothing. Smoke from his cigarette curled in his hair. He leaned on the gate with folded arms, then knocked some ash from his cigarette and spat a thread of tobacco from his tongue.

'You could have killed someone, Mr. Marwick.'

'My land, Hedges. I can fell any trees I like.'

They spoke in mild tones like men discussing the weather.

'You can't stop us using the river.'

'Is that what you think?' He took his cigarette out and blew a smoke ring.

Hedges smiled. It hurt the bruise on his face. 'There's another thing. I don't like what you did last night.'

'To your Hun lady, eh? What are you going to do about it, Hedges?'

In answer, Hedges took off his jacket. He folded it and laid it on the ground. He unfastened his watch from his waistcoat and put it on top of the jacket. Then he faced Marwick. He put his left leg forward and doubled his fists and stood waiting. There was something comic in it, he knew, but he would not let himself think about it. He saw disbelief on Marwick's face. It turned to greed. Marwick stubbed out his cigarette on the gatepost.

'You want to fight me, Hedges? This'll be good.' He opened the gate and came through. His face grinned, he worked his shoulders, splayed his hands. He meant to hurt Hedges.

Noel and Phil were watching from the gorse patch in the hollow. They had slipped away from the other boys, and crept across the paddocks out of sight.

Noel said, 'Marwick's too big. He'll murder Clippy.'

'Clippy knows what he's doing.'

'We should get the police.'

'No,' Phil said. He reached into the gorse and pulled an old fence baton free. 'If he gets him down, I'll bash him with this.'

They both called a warning as Marwick attacked. Hedges did not need it. He stood his ground, faced Marwick, struck him in the face with his left hand, and stepped back. Marwick looked as if he had walked into a wall. He touched his mouth and brought his fingers away smeared with blood. He could not believe it. He gave a strangled shout and ran at Hedges. Hedges hit him with his left again, stood Marwick still, and crossed a short punch with his right and knocked him down. Marwick lay stunned on the grass. He raised himself on his elbow and looked toward Hedges with unfocused eyes.

Hedges looked at his fists. He wiped them on his trousers. He blinked, as though waking up. 'Perhaps that can settle it, Mr. Marwick. I hope we can behave like adults now.' He saw the heat rise in Marwick's face, in his eyes, and he said, 'Well, I'm sorry.' He picked up his watch and jacket and walked away. Marwick, on his elbow, watched him go. He climbed to his knees. His fingers dug into his thighs. Whimpers of rage came from his mouth.

Hedges walked down the road to the bridge. He saw

Noel and Phil running in the paddock and waited for them.

'I told you boys to go back to school.'

'We thought you might need help, Sir.'

'Did he get you?'

'I'm all right.' Hedges was gruff.

'You were great, Sir.'

'Where did you learn to box?'

'I used to spar with Young Griffo.'

'Who's he?'

'Never mind. I'm sorry you boys saw that. It won't solve anything. It'll make him worse.'

'It makes you feel good, though,' Phil said.

'I feel like a crocodile.' They crossed the bridge. 'We'll have to stop using the river.'

'Aw, Sir!'

'That's not fair, Sir,' Noel said.

'At least until the police do something about him.'

They went on down the road. The other boys had gone from sight, but girls ran from the path to Girlie's Hole. Two ran in the direction of town, but the third, Melva Dyer, saw Hedges. She started towards him, dust puffing under her feet.

'What is it? What's the matter?' Hedges yelled.

Melva came up panting, caught his arms. 'Mrs. Marwick's drowning,' she gasped.

◆

Kitty and Irene had swum halfway to the rapids. They rested by the bank, holding on to knobs of rock, with their legs trailing in deep water.

'Is she watching?' But Mrs. Bolton was busy with the non-swimmers, so they climbed on to the bank. Kitty went four or five feet up and got ready to dive. As Mrs. Bolton looked, she launched herself and cut into the water with no splash.

'Kitty!'

For a long time she did not come up. Irene began to worry, and on the shingle down-river, Mrs. Bolton put her hand to her breast. Then Kitty surfaced in the deep part of the pool below the rapids.

'Kitty! Kitty! I told you not to dive.'

Kitty was deafened by the noise of water. She put her finger to her ear. 'I can't hear, Mrs. Bolton.'

Irene teetered and pretended to lose her balance. She flopped head first into the water and came straight up.

'Irene!'

'I slipped, Mrs. Bolton.' She dog-paddled back to the bank and caught hold. She grinned at Kitty. Then, by the rapids, where they tumbled in the narrow part of the chute, she saw Mrs. Marwick come from the bush. Her face was turned to Kitty and had an expression of terrible fear.

'Lucy!' she shrieked. The cry came sharp through the noise of water. Kitty jerked her head round. She saw Mrs. Marwick reach for her, saw her step blindly into the rapids. They knocked her over, pulled her down. She tumbled in white water — arm, shoe, wide-open eyes. Then she floated into the deep, with air ballooning in her dress. Her face kept slipping under, coming up. She looked about for Kitty, reaching out. Her grey hair trailed and filled her mouth.

Kitty swam towards her. She grabbed her as she sank and

kept away from her gripping hands. Irene came up. 'Lift her head. Keep it out of the water.' They pulled Mrs. Marwick down-river to the shingle bank. Other girls swam to help. When their feet touched bottom, they bobbed along, floating the old lady on her back. Irene held her head out of the water. They lifted Mrs. Marwick and carried her over the shingle to the grass. Her sodden dress trailed on the ground.

'Put her here,' Mrs. Bolton said.

Irene looked up. 'I think she's dead.'

'Does anyone know artificial respiration?'

'She's breathing,' Kitty said. 'Only just.'

Mrs. Bolton sent girls running for help. Then they stood in a ring round Mrs. Marwick.

'You girls in bathing suits get dressed. Oh, Mr. Hedges, thank heavens! Go away Miller, go away Wix. There's girls changing here.'

Hedges knelt beside Mrs. Marwick. He hooked his finger in her mouth and brought her false teeth out. 'Get her on her stomach.' With Kitty and Irene he rolled her over. He put her head on one side, made sure her tongue was clear, and started artificial respiration. 'Noel, Phil, ambulance.'

'I sent some girls for that,' Mrs. Bolton said.

'Good.' He pressed on Mrs. Marwick's back, relaxed. 'Go back to the house. Call Mr. Marwick.' The boys started off. 'Don't get close to him.'

Noel and Phil ran up the path. They ran along the road and over the bridge, then climbed a fence and cut across the paddock. Marwick was gone from in front of the croquet lawn. The house was silent.

'What'll we do?'

'Biff a stone on the roof.'

But they called Marwick's name, and called again; and the door sprang back and Marwick came out with a lump of firewood in his hand. He jumped down from the veranda and ran over the lawn.

'Your mother's drowning, Mr. Marwick.'

'She fell in Girlie's Hole.'

Marwick stopped as though he had been punched in the face again. He staggered sideways. The lump of firewood fell from his hand. Then he started forward, opened the gate, came into the paddock. The boys moved ahead of him, keeping a ten-yard distance.

'She isn't dead,' Phil said.

'The ambulance is coming.'

Marwick started to run. His face looked as if he had already run many miles. Noel and Phil let him go past. He went without seeing. They fell in behind, and jogged along. When they crossed the bridge they saw an ambulance drawn up by the path to Girlie's Hole. The back door was gaping and Irene and Kitty, wet-haired, in their clothes, stood beside it. Ambulance men brought Mrs. Marwick from the path on a stretcher. Hedges and Mrs. Bolton came behind.

'No staring, girls. Come along now,' Mrs. Bolton said.

The ambulance men put the stretcher in. Then Marwick arrived, and Hedges said, 'She's all right, Mr. Marwick. These girls got her out.'

Marwick took no notice. He tried to climb into the ambulance but tripped on the step and one of the men had to help him inside. He knelt by the stretcher and moaned. He pushed wet hair from his mother's brow. 'Ma?'

Hedges said quietly, 'Mr. Marwick.' He held out Mrs. Marwick's teeth.

Marwick turned his head. His lips came back in a snarl. A red flicker showed in his eyes. 'You did this. You and those kids.' He turned away, and it was as if a flame had been blown out. 'Ma? Please, look at me, Ma.' He stroked her face.

Hedges gave the false teeth to one of the ambulance men. The other closed the door and the ambulance drove away.

CHAPTER TWELVE

The White Lady

THAT SHOULD HAVE been enough for one day. But to Phil it seemed a huge wheel was turning and would not stop. He seemed to hear the rumbling sound it made and a cracking of bones under its rim.

He sat with Noel on the Wixes' front fence and watched Irene playing the piano. The music came through the open window. Kitty stood beside her, turning the pages.

'You could have come tonight if it hadn't been for Charmy-Barmy,' Noel said.

'Doesn't matter. She really belts it out on that piano.'

'She's a skite.'

'She helped pull that old dame Marwick out.'

'Yeah. They'll probably get a medal for saving her.'

'Who wants medals? I wish I could box like Clippy.'

'He's getting spliced. To old Ma Stauffel.'

'Kitty said.' That too seemed part of the wheel turning. 'Did you see Marwick's eyes? I reckon he'll have a go at Clippy.'

'Burn his house?'

'Or murder him. He could murder that Stauffel. He'll do something tonight, that's what I reckon. We should watch him.'

'How?'

Irene stopped playing and the girls came into the garden.

'Phil thinks Marwick will try to do something to Clippy tonight,' Noel said.

'We should watch his house.'

'Too risky. He'd kill us if he found us.'

'We could write another letter to the police,' Irene said.

'Sure, and sign it Miss Perez.'

'Well, what can we do?'

'Play him a lullaby. Put him to sleep.'

'Quit it,' Phil said. Their quarrelling seemed very childish to him. 'We'll watch his house. But we don't have to do it from up close.' Their eyes fastened on him. He felt he was on the stage again, playing New Zealand — but this time he was sure of himself. He made them lean close, and told his plan.

◆

He went home, but did not stay. Already he seemed to have left the place behind. He had not been unhappy there, or happy either, but it had been his, and now he had to live with other people. The Wixes. Clippy Hedges probably. If he got spliced that meant the Frau, the piano teacher. At least she looked as if she knew how to cook. But they'd better not try to teach him the piano. Learning about the stars was enough.

He took down the picture of Halley's Comet and put it on the table so he wouldn't forget it when he picked up his

stuff tomorrow. Then he gave a last look round the place —
his table, his chair, his stove — and left it and walked into
town, chewing a bit of bread he'd grabbed from the shelf.
For a while he hung about the station, watching recruits get
on the train for Trentham Camp. They kissed their wives
and girlfriends. Phil envied them — not the kissing, the going away.

He watched the red carriages roll out and fold off one by
one round the bend. Then he ran to the cathedral and
climbed the steps and saw the train cross the river bridge
and go like a worm into the tunnel on the other side. Its
smoke flattened out and was sucked in. Everything was still.
The sky turned red, the estuary pink. At the rivermouth,
men in dinghies were netting flounder. Jessop seemed
strange, full of buildings he did not recognize. The cathedral tower leaned over him. Darkness spread like water
through the town, showing caves and corners he did not
know.

He walked down the main street and turned off at the
square, went by the fire station, by the park, and passed up
Dargie Street by the burned-out stables. That helped bring
the real Jessop back. The bakehouse was dark, but he remembered Mr. Wix's pies and his mouth filled with saliva.
He spat in the gutter and started to run. His bare feet made
a drumming on the footbridge and the boards trembled. All
the corners were full of shadows, but he rose above the dark
as he climbed Settlers Hill. The air seemed thinner. The sky
was like a washed blue basin. Stars came out as he stood and
watched.

The observatory was silent on top of the hill. It was, Phil
thought, like a buried skull, half out of the ground. He had

never been frightened of the dark but felt nervous as he found the key. Inside, he closed the door softly. He took a box of matches from his pocket and struck one. The light did not travel far. He saw the telescope, up on its back legs like a praying mantis. An optic nerve, Clippy had said, but that seemed to make it less scientific, more spooky.

The match went out. He struck another. He opened the window and took the small telescope from the table. The second match went out but he did not need light any longer. He focused the telescope. It was hard in the dark. Only one light showed in Marwick's farmhouse. It was square, like the page of a book. He saw a table in a room, with something red on it — a vase of flowers. Now and then a shadow crossed the table. Phil knew that was Edgar Marwick.

He sat a long time watching, changing now and then from eye to eye. Once he saw Marwick's hands. They lay still on the wood. Later on they set down a plate and knife and fork.

A tapping came on the door. He felt his heart bounce like a ball.

'Noel?'

'Can I come in?'

'Yeah. Close the door.'

Noel came in like a rat in the dark. He seemed to snuffle at the room. 'It's dark in here. I brought a candle.'

'I'm not scared of the dark.'

'The window's away from town. No one'll see.'

'Marwick might.'

Noel struck a match and lit the candle. 'I'll keep it over here on the table. Have you seen him?'

'In the kitchen. Getting his tea.'

'I brought you a pie.'

'Thanks.'

'And a blanket.'

'On the table. Watch while I eat this.'

Noel came to the window and took the telescope. He found the lighted window in the house. 'Can't see much. You should use the big one.'

'I'd have to open the roof. Clippy wouldn't like it, anyway.' He wolfed the pie. 'You better go. Even I'm not supposed to be here.'

Noel handed the telescope back. 'Do you reckon he'll do anything?'

'Dunno.' Marwick was sitting at the table again. His hands lay on either side of his empty plate. Phil did not like their stillness. Sooner or later they would do something.

'I'll leave my window open,' Noel said.

'OK.'

'The girls are staying awake. Trying to.'

Phil said nothing. He could not connect Irene and Kitty, waiting for an adventure, with Edgar Marwick down in the house. It was nothing like that any more. It was dangerous and he was afraid. Noel crept out and closed the door behind him. Phil pulled the blanket over his shoulders and settled down to watch. The hours went by. Several times he dozed but the window was alight when he looked again, and Marwick was still sitting at the table. Once, though, food was on his plate. He did not eat; his hands lay on the wood. Phil realized he must have dozed for a fairly long time. He looked at the candle. It was burned down over half way.

Later, when it had guttered out, he strained his ears to hear the Post Office clock. A single chime came. He did not know whether it was alone or the end of a sequence. He guessed that it was after midnight though.

At last Marwick moved . . .

◆

He did not know why he was sitting there. Nothing made any connection with the movements in his mind, which were a dance of flame and shadow. Table, chair, plate and food, knife, fork, the stove, the walls, the floor, had no substance until he touched them. They struck him then as a kind of insult, an attempt by someone to deny that what went on in his head had importance. Yet he came back and took the fork and moved a piece of meat on his plate. He speared it, lifted it to his mouth. It was cold. He chewed a while but could not swallow and spat the meat on to his plate. It seemed that if he took it into himself he would betray the flames that danced like figures in his head.

He stood up and went to the stove and opened the firebox. The clock ticked on the mantelpiece. Suddenly it gave a single chime. In another room, another clock also chimed. He picked up the poker and stirred the cold ashes, trying to find a sign of life. The greyness inside the stove was another insult. Suddenly it was more than he could take. He stood up and looked around and saw the plate of congealed stew on the table. He took two strides at it and smashed the poker down on the plate. Food and broken china flew everywhere. He hit the vase of withered flowers, making it explode. Then he hurled the poker into the piles of plates and cups on the shelf. He grabbed a kerosene lamp, turned up the wick, and lit it with a match. Then he strode through the house to his mother's room and pulled open drawers. He tore out clothes in handfuls until he found what he wanted — a red woolen scarf. He wrapped it round his head like a turban, knotted it, and went out to the yard. He put the lamp on the chopping block and started hurling lumps of firewood out of the lean-to shed. In a moment he came to what he wanted.

◆

Phil could not make out what the red thing was on Marwick's head. Not a balaclava, not a hat — but he had no doubt what it meant. The man had moved too far from the circle of light for him to see what he was doing, but lumps of wood came flying from the woodshed, and when Marwick came out with sack and can, he was not surprised. What surprised him was the speed with which things happened. Marwick pushed the can into the sack, already stuffed with rags Phil supposed, and shouldered it, and set off into the night. He simply vanished. The lamp burned on the chopping block.

Phil threw off his blanket. He closed the window and put the telescope on the table. Then he ran down the path from Settlers Hill, through the park, over the footbridge, and sped through the streets of Jessop until he came to Noel's house. He vaulted the stone fence instead of going in by the gate. At the back of the house he found an open window, and pushed the stirring curtain aside and touched Noel's face on the pillow. Noel gave a yelp.

'Quiet,' Phil whispered.

'What? Phil?'

'He's coming. He's got benzine and rags. And a red thing round his head.'

Noel got out of bed. He grabbed his clothes. 'What time is it?'

'One o'clock. He was smashing things with a poker.'

The door opened and Kitty came in.

'Go back to bed,' Noel whispered.

'Is it Marwick?'

'He's coming. With his stuff,' Phil said.

'Wait for us.' She was gone.

'They've been taking turns to stay awake,' Noel said.

'We'll need them to get the police. I'll wait by Dargie's.' He went back up the path and across the lawn and over the fence and ran down the street to the empty section. He waited in the bakehouse alley. Noel and Kitty and Irene arrived, shivering. They had pulled on clothes and Irene was wearing slippers. Noel and Kitty had bare feet.

'He's got to come over the footbridge,' Phil said. 'So that's where we'll wait. Underneath. When he's gone over we follow him.'

They ran to the bridge and scrambled down the bank and crawled underneath. 'One of us should go for the police.'

'Not till we know where he's going. We've got to catch him in the act.'

Light from a gas lamp came through the planking and striped their faces. The sound of running water came from the river. A sour smell of urine filled the air. 'Someone's been using this as a dunny.'

'Shut up.' Phil was leaning out. 'I hear his feet.' He ducked back. They huddled close to the ground, deep in the angle where bridge and bank met. On the other side of the river feet crunched on gravel. Then the bridge began to drum. Marwick came across. He passed over them, his feet only inches from their heads. The strips of light flickered on their faces. Gravel crunched again and the sound moved off.

Phil leaned out. He crept up the bank and raised his head to the level of the road. Marwick had moved into the dark place between two lights, but he grew distinct for a moment, his head seemed to burn like an ember. Then he was gone, with a sudden turn left.

'He's gone up Leckie's Lane.'

'Where to?'

'Not Frau Stauffel's.'

'It must be Hedges'.'

'Come on. He'll get away.'

They ran to the corner and peered up Leckie's Lane. It ran between high wooden walls and was lit by a lamp at each end. The middle was black, and Marwick seemed to climb out of a pit. Again the ember-glow of his head, as though brought alive by someone blowing, then his black bent body, the hump of the sack on his back. He vanished again.

'It's Hedges' place all right.'

They ran up the lane. Along the road the lime trees stood in front of the school. They were like a row of green gas balloons, but the street was empty. Nothing moved except a sudden cat that leaped on a wall.

'Where's he gone?'

'If we lose him they'll never believe us.'

'That cat was in the school,' Kitty said.

They ran to the gate and climbed into the grounds. The school was dark, although windows glittered here and there. Every day they sat in it, but now it seemed a threatening place. A shadow made a sudden hump-backed flit along a wall.

'There he is.'

'He's cutting through to Clippy's.'

'It's quicker down the street.'

Fast, soft-footed, they crossed the football field and the playground. They went up the side of the school and looked into the back field. It seemed like a pool of water, black and deep. Marwick was somewhere in it, under the surface.

'Where's he gone?'

Then Kitty said, 'It isn't Clippy's place. He's going to burn the school,' and they knew she was right. There was no other place for Marwick to go. A soft thump came from inside the building.

'We're too late to stop him.'

They ran along the back of the school. A window was open like a mouth. It seemed to them, all four, that if they went inside they would be swallowed. It opened out of safety into the dark.

Phil gripped the sill. 'I'm going in.' He pulled himself up, swung his leg. He was gone. Noel followed. And Kitty too climbed up and dropped inside. She felt as if she was up to her neck in water. She did not know which way the boys had gone. 'Get the police,' she whispered to Irene.

'No. I'm coming.'

Her slippers scuffed on the sill. She stood by Kitty, clutching her arm. 'Where have they gone?'

Phil and Noel had crept along the corridor to the staff-room, but Marwick had gone further on. He was in Hedges' classroom, and as the boys approached they heard a scrape of desk-legs on the floor. Marwick was dragging furniture into the middle of the room.

They turned and padded quickly back to the window.

'He's building a fire. No time for the police.' Phil grabbed the girls by their shoulders. 'Get up in the belfry and ring the bell, hard as you can. We'll try and stop him.'

The girls hurried away. Their feet whispered on the steps. Phil and Noel went back down the corridor. They heard the gritty sound of a can being opened. It terrified them. Liquid splashed, and grunts of pleasure came from Edgar Marwick. Noel and Phil, looking in at the door, saw his eyes glint. The last of the benzine gurgled out. Marwick put down the can. It made a soft boom. He took a box of matches from his pocket. The boys crept close. They stood behind him, close enough to touch his shoulder.

Marwick struck a match. Light colored him, showed his scarf-wrapped head and yellow face. The match burned down half its length. Then Noel did the only thing he could think of. He leaned past Marwick's elbow and blew it out. Phil jumped into the dark at Marwick's arm and knocked the box of matches from his hand. He sprang after it, felt among the wet lids of desks, and had the box, and yelled, 'I've got his matches.' In the same instant the school-bell started ringing. It clapped and sang with marvelous clarity, sending out its sound over sleeping Jessop.

But Marwick was not finished. He sprang for the door. He found the light switch, and the room leaped out, blinding the boys. He faced them and his eyes narrowed down and focused on them. A look of greed came on his face. He spoke heavily, as though he had reached an end at last.

'Got you.'

Noel and Phil crouched behind the desks. 'The police are coming,' Noel yelled.

Marwick took no notice. He reached out with one arm and closed the door. It made a heavy thud and the wind from it flapped Clippy's charts on the wall.

'Got you. Now.' He walked to Clippy's table and flipped it on its side with one hand. It was a kauri table with turned legs and Clippy was very proud of it. Marwick seized the leg projecting at him. He took it in two hands and his jacket grew tight on his shoulders, his throat and face swelled and grew red, as he wrenched, once, twice . . . The glue and dowelling snapped with a gunshot crack, and the leg came off. Marwick faced the boys with the huge round club in his hands. He walked at them, and the bell in the belfry seemed to clang faster, encouraging him.

Marwick charged, swinging his club. It crashed down on a desk and split the lid. Noel and Phil were away, Noel just out of range of the blow. He felt its wind, and cried to Phil, 'He's going to kill us.'

Marwick charged again. The boys ran round the pile of desks. They kept ahead of him, but could not run for the door. In the time it would take to open it he would have them.

Then Marwick stopped. He began flinging desks aside with one hand, breaking down the pile.

'Throw stuff,' Phil yelled. He picked up a slate and threw, then a heavy book. He threw a compass and the point went into Marwick's jacket and jabbed his arm. Marwick gave a howl and leaped at the desks, trying to charge right over them. His foot slipped in a puddle of benzine and he crashed down on his back. The force of it shook the floor.

Noel and Phil saw their chance. They kept clear of his arms, as long as rakes, and ran for the door, and along the corridor to the window.

The bell still rang. Like some great bird, the belfry kept on singing its song, and Phil screamed up the stairs, 'That's enough!'

'Too late,' Noel cried. Marwick came lurching from the classroom. 'Up. We'll lock ourselves in.'

They ran up the stairs into the belfry. Irene and Kitty were on the rope, pulling as though they meant to jerk the bell down from its tower. Wild-eyed, they stared at the boys. Moonlight, slanting through the slats, lit their faces.

'Keep ringing,' Phil cried. He slammed the door and pushed in the bolt. Noel had run to the window. He looked down at the playing field. 'No one's coming.'

'They'll come. Keep on that bell.'

Then the door rattled. Marwick, on the other side, was jerking at the handle. He beat on it with his fist.

'Jam some desks against it.' Phil and Noel hauled a broken desk across the floor. But the door gave a monstrous boom. Wood cracked about the bolt. 'He's hitting it with his club. He'll break it down.' They watched helplessly. Marwick hit again. The bracing plank split down its length and borer dust floated in the air. They could not believe a human was strong enough for this.

Then Noel cried, 'Miss Perez!' It was as if she had reached out from her cupboard and plucked the hair on the nape of his neck. He sprang at the cupboard. He found the key hanging on its nail, and opened the door, and seemed to feel her fingers reach for him. She was luminous, alive in her coffin. She grinned at him.

Phil came to his side. They pulled her out and her dry arms folded round their necks. She rattled, she chattered and seemed to laugh. The door bulged with a blow of the club.

'Put her here.'

They stood her facing the door. Marwick hit once again, and rammed with his shoulder, and burst into the room. His feet caught the top step and threw him on his knees. When he looked up, Miss Perez was standing over him. The bell stopped ringing. To Marwick, she came into being with the silence. Her bones were bright in the inky blackness. Nothing existed outside her. Slowly she opened her hands. Jerkily, possessively, raised her arms. She reached for him. Marwick screamed. He covered his face. He left the table leg and shuffled into a corner. The wall stopped him. He squatted there and watched her over his elbow. His eyes leaked tears down his face.

Irene and Kitty ran from the belfry. They climbed out the window and ran round to the front of the school. Men were advancing from the gate, with Hedges and McCaa in the lead. The girls ran to them.

'It's Mr. Marwick. In the belfry.'

'He tried to burn the school.'

'Is anyone else in there?'

'Noel and Phil.'

'All right. You two stay here.'

Hedges had a bunch of keys. He opened the school door and McCaa pushed him aside and ran in. Hedges followed. They ran up the stairs to the belfry. McCaa also cried out on seeing Miss Perez, but he noticed Noel and Phil kneeling behind her, and turned where she was looking and saw

Edgar Marwick. He was sitting in the broken bats, as deep in the corner as he could go. Big man though he was, he seemed as small as a child, with hands shielding the lower part of his face, and knees drawn up, and eyes dark with horror.

Hedges said, 'Put her away now, boys. Put her away.'

He went by McCaa's side to Edgar Marwick and touched his shoulder. 'She's gone now. She can't get you.' He eased the knotted scarf from Marwick's head and dropped it on the floor and helped McCaa lift him. They took the fire-raiser past the desks and through the broken door and out of the belfry.

Noel and Phil locked Miss Perez in her cupboard.

◆

Kitty and Irene waited on the steps. They watched McCaa bring Edgar Marwick out. They saw his wet cheeks and trembling mouth. His eyes saw nothing; they seemed blind.

McCaa led him away by one arm.

Hedges came out of the school with Noel and Phil. Phil carried Edgar Marwick's club. Hedges took it from him. 'Leave that, Phil.' He leaned it on the wall, and put his arms round the girls' shoulders.

'I'll take you home.'

They went down the steps, Hedges, Irene, Kitty, with Noel on one side and Phil on the other. Men in shirts and braces parted to let them through. Wix and Chalmers came running in the gate.

Marwick went out. McCaa put him into his car and drove away.

Noel found he had the fire-raiser's scarf trailing from his

hand. He did not remember picking it up, and did not want it. He let it drop.

As they walked on it lay behind them at the foot of the steps, like a pile of embers in the dark.